The Sky Alone

Wolf Tinker

and

Joanna Erbach

Tapolith Books

An Imprint of Studio Pyraxis

DEDICATION

To Pyraxis, who opened the door to the Dreaming.

To my godmother Jeanette, who believes in me.

TABLE OF CONTENTS

CHAPTER 1
His Side of the Mountain

The sound of someone coughing awakened me. Someone had found me. It could only be rsakk or nethik, and the nethik had agreed to leave me alone. Sighing, I turned on my side, hoping my wings would knock him off the narrow ledge that was the entrance to my camp. I was rewarded by the sound of rocks falling and the scrabble of claws on the cliff. I smiled because I knew that then I could sleep.

A second cough wiped the smile from my thoughts and drew a second sigh from me. I shifted back to nok, sat up in my human form. The ledge was still bare. A frigid wind blew, and I heard the cough again. Someone was trying to pronounce my name.

"(Cough cough)," the grehti have need of you."

9

I jumped up and went to the edge. It's not good to mess with the grehti, especially if one of them had made the effort to climb up here. A priest could make trouble for me.

I had to lean over the edge to find him – he was clinging with his lizard claws to the side of the cliff and shivering as icy winds dug under his scales. He had grehti markings, left there by his robes when he shifted. Those made the bands of color around his legs, neck and midsection. I did not recognize the tribe. If he was a priest, he should have red or white or blue marks. His were grey and brown and white. Odd for a rsakk.

"(Cough cough)," he said again, and there was a hint of desperation in his voice. I rolled my eyes and leapt off the side of the cliff.

It was the only way to save him. It was likely that he had shifted to climb, but with the threat of falling off the cliff, his instincts would not have allowed him to shift back to nok so I could pull him up. So he fell, and in time I caught him in my claws. K'g'hrah are the largest shapeshifters on Karn, and rsakk the second largest. The bodies of the rsakk make it easy for a k'g'hrah to pluck them from almost anywhere, though it is easier if they are falling.

I deposited this fellow on the ledge and then landed beside him. He shifted to nok almost immediately. It was amusing to see the look of terror on his face as I tucked my wings. But I didn't knock him off again. I too shifted to nok – it was the only way to get into the sheltered part of the cave, where he would have a reasonable chance of not freezing to death before I started a fire.

He was grehti so probably I would get in trouble. I had been in that kind of trouble in the past. But since I had come to the mountain I had not gotten into trouble at all. The priests, like the nethik, had agreed to leave me alone. I decided to be nice to this one since it might help there to be less trouble.

He said nothing while I worked on the fire, so I thought about where I should go, because now I would have to leave.

The place where he found me was a good camp. It was a place where the sky sang to me even when I was not singing to it with my flute. It was a place from which I could look down on the other mountains. It was rocky and steep so that even the traders could not climb up to it. But the rsakk priest had come. That meant it was no longer private. That meant I would have to leave.

The fire was done and the rsakk sat shivering in front of it. His heavy tunic might insulate him against the heat of the badlands, but it was too thin for the mountains and he had gotten it wet. I had furs, but he refused them. I shrugged and sat down. It wasn't cold to me. Come the cold season I might use one or two of the furs, but it was summer and I didn't need anything other than what I wore, a red string with a bead. The rsakk was wearing a tunic, pants, and I was willing to bet he'd left a cloak behind when he shifted to his lizard shape.

He coughed again; I guessed the cough was the best pronunciation he could manage for my name. A cough and a sneeze would have been more accurate, but at that time he would not manage it because his teeth were knocking together fast and hard. Nonetheless he tried again.

"Kgh'jsh of Cnieren," he repeated, "the grehti have need of your services."

"I live to serve the Mother." I gave him the proper reply with respect, and I served him some ruka, which I'd set to thaw while I built the fire.

"I am Zev," he said. He smiled and my mood fell down a bit, because I saw a mouthful of filed teeth – royalty, then, as well as a priest.

"Sent from Ak-Shamalim," he said, which did not improve my mood but did explain some things.

Ak-Shamalim explained why he was unprepared for the cold, and Ak-Shamalim forecast a hot, dry assignment. Grehti meant one which I would not be able to refuse. It meant there would be an assignment for which I would be paid well, but from which I might be lucky to escape with my feathers intact.

CHAPTER 2
The Storyteller

It was the tradition of the shashigai, the tribe of storytellers, to send men to find the stories of all the races and keep them. The stories brought back were woven into tapestries, memorized or painted on sacred cave walls. Some of the stories were kept without telling, because the shashigai were also information brokers, and the information they held both kept their tribe wealthy and in relative safety from overt attack.

The storyteller slapped away still more of the tiny biting bugs and pulled his cloak tighter around him. He was from a place far to the south of where he was now, and not only was it cold here, but there were things in the air and on the ground that could exist only in a climate wetter than his. There were things that crawled and bit and sucked blood that could not be seen until the damage was done. The storyteller was cold and wet, and he missed his home. He didn't miss the heat so much as the dry air. The air in the forest seemed to catch in his lungs and more than a few times gave him the sensation that he was smothering. The trees were tall and full, and there were places where it was as dark as after sunset. He'd heard stories about speritu demons lurking in these woods, but he hoped that they wouldn't be out during the day. Speritu hated light. No one had ever encountered a sperith in a place where there was bright light, whether from fire or from the sun.

The little caravan of men with their supplies had been walking through the woods for most of the day. The trail was in a high place; not only that but it was narrow and hard to see. Even the guides had stopped a couple of times to argue about which way to go. They were natives of the area, but from a different race, one that did not have good relations with his own; in fact his people routinely enslaved them in his part of the world. It was possible that they were leading him poorly on purpose, but there was no reason for that. The storyteller had no specific timetable and the village of the two men leading the group had no specific argument with the storyteller's tribe.

At last the group came upon a change in terrain. It was not so much a change in the plants and trees as what was underfoot. The ground had been soft beneath their feet, but the softness was from pine needles and rotted leaves, which did not feel good to the storyteller's feet. Now in addition to everything else there were stones and pebbles and mud.

The trees still stretched up into the sky; they seemed as tall as the buttes and bluffs of the storyteller's home in the badlands. They blocked a clear view of the sky. Although they let light in, they were still close enough together to make the storyteller feel a little claustrophobic. Some of the trees were as big around as houses. The storyteller lived in a caravan with wagons and tents, and so the trees seemed even larger to him. Sunlight sifted through the trees and lighted their way, but it did not warm them. Pine needles and wet leaves slipped between his feet and the soles of his sandals and made him feel continuously damp. The soft ground and the closeness of the trees cut sound off in places, while in others some trick of the terrain made noises echo as if in a cave. Small bushes, some bristling with long, sharp thorns, snagged and pulled at the storyteller's clothes. Large ferns, wet with dew, brushed his cloak with water, making it feel heavy and cold.

He'd refused to trade for local garb because those clothes were more suited to the shape of the natives. The thought made him grin, even though he still shivered a little from the cold; he was imagining himself in nethik boots when he shifted shapes – the magic was such that one's clothes became integrated with the sacred shape. He was imagining what his back legs and claws would look like with nethik "gloves." The nethik looked fine with their back legs and hooves integrated with the boots – the boots changed to a layer of warm fur. Not so useful for a lizard shape running through the rocky, sandy soil of the badlands. He shook himself as he thought of sand clinging to fur, and what would happen inside the boots when he shifted back to his nok, human form with all that sand in them. The thought made him shiver, which made him remember that his feet were cold.

The boots would have been useful, and warm. Now he realized with regret that if the need had arisen he could have taken them off before shifting.

The change in the terrain had made him further regret having kept his sandals; now in addition to the wet leaves and sharp pine needles, small stones and mud insinuated themselves between the soles of his feet and the soles of the sandals. Gritty things worked their way between his toes. The cold made the tiny hard things seem even harder. At last he had to stop. The storyteller gave in and allowed the nethik guides to wrap his feet in strips of animal skin. The skins were sticky and damp but at least they were warm.

He went back to musing about what would happen if some danger threatened. He'd have to drop the nethik pack if he shifted; it would press on his crest and interfere with his movement. The straps might hamper his breathing too, if he were in shape. Rsakk were built for battle; anything that obstructed breathing would reduce his ability to gather and ignite the internal gasses that rsakk used to make fire.

The pack straps were leather, braided into some kind of stretchy strap, but he doubted that they would be long enough to wrap around his body without binding or tangling his legs. He shrugged off concern. In nethik territory, it was unlikely that there would be any danger that called for him to change.

The cold was the worst threat, and the closeness of the trees. After they left the forest, the increasing height of the mountains would add to the threat of the cold. Here, the nethik could not be enslaved as they were in the south. At the first opportunity they slipped in among the trees and vanished. In the woods, they were as elusive as the storyteller's current prey.

The guides and some of the pack carriers were from the nethik race; the storyteller's caravan was based in a land where these people were slaves and served the rsakk, the shape to which the storyteller belonged. Here in the woods the nethik had none of the disadvantages they had in the badlands. The narrow, almost invisible trails allowed them to defend themselves. He wondered if some of the stories of demons dropping from trees were actually about nethik.

The group stopped for a meal break, and the storyteller got a chance to take a more measured look around him. The area he was in had been described to him. It had been an accurate description. The forest had continued from the village up into the mountains, where the temperature dropped and remained so even in the sun. It was several days' climb to the place where the keegrah had been reported to make his camp.

The storyteller's first stop before venturing into the mountains had been to visit the nethik storyteller who lived in the village near this mountain.

The nethik storyteller, whose name was Nishom, sat near the fire in front of his leather tent and shared a drink of ruka with the rsakk storyteller, whose name was Zev. The ruka of the nethik was made from roots and fruit fermented together with spices. It was unusual but good, especially since the night was cold, and the ruka had been heated.

"The one you seek is in the keegrah mountains," Nishom had told him, "Perhaps you should send a keegrah to find him."

"I heard that the only one he will talk to is a rsakk."

"I have heard that too," said Nishom, "But he talks to us when he comes here. It is good that you are rsakk. His friend was rsakk, so he is friendly to rsakk. But I think that even so he will not talk to you."

"But I am rsakk."

"You are also grehti, and he does not like grehti."

"But I am from Ak-Shamalim."

Nishom snorted.

"Your caravan camps near there. He does not like to talk. But Ak-Shamalim might make him listen."

"I have this," said Zev, and he pulled from beneath his tunic a pouch. Out into his hand tumbled a red gem, which seemed to dance with its own flame in the firelight.

Nishom shook his head.

"This one, you will not bribe. He does not like things like that."

"Ah," said Zev, returning the stone to its pouch, "I may have other, more valuable things to trade with him."

He did not elaborate, and the nethik raised an eyebrow, but said nothing. It was an agreement among the shashigai, that if there was a story to be told, it would be told to the ones who needed to hear it. If indeed Zev did find the keegrah in the mountains, then the story would come back to Nishom in one form or another.

"I can guide you to the mountain," said Nishom, "but after a time my guides will not be able to follow you. In their nok shape they will not be able to climb the mountain, even with ropes. And after a point, they will refuse. On this mountain, we respect the demons."

"You do not kill speritu? Even when they kill you?"

"We have not had a sperith kill anyone in these parts for moons and moons." He looked pointedly at the shashigai in his grehti robes with rsakk embroidery.

The shashigai shrugged.

"Not all rsakk follow all rsakk customs," he said, "I can respect your demons so long as they do not threaten me."

"You will not need the guides when you get as far as the cliffs. If you see a demon, your fire will protect you.

The only dangers are the rocks and the cold. Your claws will serve you well, even if your scales cannot."

"You are sure about the mountain?"

"He trades with us sometimes, and he comes here when he has needs. He does not like to change his camp, so it is likely that he is still there. We have seen him flying up there. Most of the other keegrah have their camps closer to Cnieren, which you will pass on your way. His is the highest and farthest away. You will need boots," said Nishom, looking at Zev's sandaled feet.

"I might have to shift," said Zev, and Nishom sighed.

"Your pride may hurt you," he said.

Nishom had told him that the guides would take him on a journey along the well-marked trail to the keegrah mining village, Cnieren. After Cnieren, the trail would not be so well-marked for two reasons. The first was that Cnieren was high enough that if one needed to get to the tops of the mountains, one could fly. Since most of the inhabitants of Cnieren were keegrah, they saw no need to develop the trails.

The other reason was that the only ones who used the trails besides the occasional trader were the nethik. Most rsakk avoided the area altogether. The tirothi, though they were used to trees, lived in hotter, more jungle-like areas; they avoided the northeast cold. The nethik did not need the trails to be marked, so Zev would need guides to bring him through the trees to the point where the mountain started to go straight up.

It had taken all of the first day to get to Cnieren, and they had stopped there for the night. The elders of Cnieren had welcomed them; there was no racial antipathy between the keegrah and the nethik or the keegrah and the rsakk. The shashigai Zev had been glad of the accommodating stone huts and warm fires offered there. In some of the keegrah towns there were no such arrangements for visitors; the only fires were for the forges. The keegrah liked the cold even when they were not in shape. When they were in shape, the fur on their legs and the feathers on the rest of their bodies insulated them from the cold.

But Cnieren, for all its inaccessibility, was a trade town because of the nearby ore mines. Traders came with carts to bring away iron ore for tools and weapons. The mines were productive, so the keegrah did not have to come down from the mountain to trade, which suited their solitary nature. An individual keegrah might vanish from the mines and the town for days; this was considered normal behavior. They called it sky time, and the keegrah who took it would spend hours flying and living in a camp high above the town. The camps were developed by keegrah who used and then abandoned them. A keegrah who wanted to use one only needed to occupy it – if another keegrah came on signs of occupation, he would move on to another or make a new camp somewhere. None of the camps was in clear sight of another camp, which meant that one needed to be able to fly over the area, or know where a camp was, to get to it. The keegrah gave the highest respect to each others' privacy. This was why Zev had to find his keegrah through the nethik. The keegrah might know where another's camp was, but they would not tell.

Another change in terrain brought him out of his musings.

The group had come out by a river. The view to the top was clear from here. The guides pointed out the cliffs to him – the place to start climbing was across the river, and that part of the mountain looked to go straight up. The trees clinging to the side of the rock were much shorter than the ones through which they had been traveling. The guides had made camp on the side of the river where they were, and gone fishing. Zev crawled into the tent they erected for him and sat shivering by the fire.

The guides cooked the fish they'd caught over the fire and shared it with Zev. They said nothing of his decision not to venture into the darkening woods to hunt his own food. Zev ate the fish, and the porridge which they made from water from the river and grains they had brought with them. It left him feeling empty. He thought of his own caravan, waiting near the nethik village, and that comforted him. There they would have spiced meat rolled up in skins, and they would roast it over a fire when he returned. He would sit with his men and carve pieces of the roast meat and eat them dripping with juices. They would drink badlands ruka, made from ruka beans and spices. And then they would go home where it was warm and dry, where there was sand that sifted out of his sandals instead of things that clung to and pricked his feet.

The story for which he had paid these prices would bring him some wealth when it was woven into a tapestry. But that was not the true wealth. There were parts of the story he was seeking that would disrupt the order of things if they were made known. Those parts of the story he would deliver to the head of his tribe, in exchange for a second reward. Such secrets were dangerous for only one man to keep. The storyteller's tribe of historians understood well that not all history can be made public when it is recorded.

He yawned. The next day they would climb the hard part of the mountain, and after that, he could go home.

The next day, he awakened early, but to an empty tent. The guides were gone, and not just for hunting breakfast. He'd been warned that the nethik guides would leave suddenly; they still held to their superstitions and rituals, and they'd already told him that they would not violate the keegrah's camp or the domain of the speritu. It was likely that the figure he'd seen circling in the sky was the keegrah he sought. The nethik would not have wanted to lead him straight to the fellow.

They had left him food (and not enough of that), a sign they were not returning. The only sign of life was a bird circling high overhead. On second look, he thought he could make out keegrah features. Grumbling, the storyteller ate, then left the tent where it was (it was theirs anyway), and shifted to his rsakk shape to hunt more breakfast. After he had eaten, he would climb up to where the keegrah had his camp.

By midmorning the shashigai was empty-handed, frustrated and hungry.

They could have left him more than a bowl of cold porridge and a few dead fish. Hunting in shape was nearly impossible in the trees, and his metabolism changed as soon as he shifted, so the porridge and fish had been burned as if they actually had gone up in flames. The animals in the woods could get away from him through the trees on their own trails. He'd been unsuccessful even in nok, hunting with his spear.

Instead of continuing to hunt he shifted back to rsakk and crossed the river. The water was painfully cold and deep; in addition to that it was full of fallen logs; after being battered by them while attempting to swim, he landed somewhat further downstream from where he'd started. It took a while to get back to the starting point the guides had shown him, so that by the time he had set up ropes to try the climb in his human form, the sun was out and warming him.

The climb warmed him too, even though he was going slowly. The nethik had warned him that the trees growing on the side of the mountain could be unstable, so he'd had to check carefully where he tied his anchors. He'd left his cloak and robe at the base and was climbing in tunic and pants, so that at least the brush was not pulling at him as before. As he climbed, there were fewer trees and more rocks and mud, and finally he reached a point where there were no more trees. There were scrubby bushes that actually reminded him of the brush at home, and otherwise there were nothing but crags between his stopping point and the top of the mountain.

Time to shift. Claws would do a better job on those cracks and holds.

It was true – claws made the rocky climb a lot easier, and the sun was still warm. By the heat of it he thought it must be time for second meal. Well, he would eat twice at much at evening meal to make up for what he'd missed. Only a little further – he'd be down the mountain by sundown at this rate.

Something tickled him. It was a niggling, cold draft. And then, not a draft, but a breeze, and icy cold. A sperith? He fought back a shiver and climbed, but only a little faster. A slip would send him tumbling back down to the trees, killing him as easily as a demon's touch. He could see the edge of the cliff where the keegrah had his camp. He had not seen the keegrah go to it, but there were clear signs that someone had been there recently. There was fresh dung caught in some of the trees below, and from somewhere he caught the scent of blood – the keegrah had been feeding on fresh meat.

The breeze grew into a wind, colder still, and he allowed himself a shiver, but only after finding a good grip. Was that the sound of a flute? It must be the keegrah, who had lived for a long time in rsakk lands. The sound of it warmed the shashigai, and he couldn't figure out why until he recognized the melody. It was the fire song! On the wind above he heard a moaning and a keening cry that kept time with the flute. That sounded like a sperith! The lower wind whipped at him. Clouds covered the sun. It grew dark. He decided to climb faster.

A grueling bit of time later, things improved. The sun had moved higher in the sky. The clouds were clearing. The song of the flute had stopped, and, thankfully, so also had the keening wail of the sperith-like wind. Zev was surprised that he had not been attacked when the clouds had been thick and dark. He half wondered, half hoped that the sperith he'd heard was some distance away, possibly sucking the life out of some poor mountain animal before fleeing the wrath of the sun. The emerging sun was warm, but the lack of it had done damage to Zev. He was cold and miserable again. He sighed. If the keegrah did not have a fire, he'd make one himself.

Finally, Zev reached the top. His shape was not such that he could look over easily, so he scrambled to where he could just poke his snout over the edge. From there he could see the tips of the keegrah's wings. The keegrah's head was probably inside the cave, and by the look of it he must be sleeping. Zev hoisted himself up for a look. The huge wings were folded, and besides taking up most of the ledge, the keegrah's body completely blocked the entrance to his cave. There was little space to move onto the ledge. He dropped back down to consider what to do. He wouldn't be able to scramble up onto the ledge. He'd have to get the keegrah to move.

Zev remembered that he must call the keegrah by his chosen name. It was an odd one – not quite keegrah. The keegrah had been born in rsakk territory but here in the mountains rarely used the name given to him by his father. Nishom had told Zev that one of the ways to curry favor with this keegrah was to call him by his almost unpronounceable name – Kgh'jsh. When Nishom said it, it sounded like a cough and a sneeze. But Zev was in shape – almost impossible to sneeze – and by now was shivering to the point where all he could do was the cough.

So he hoisted himself up again, and coughed.

The keegrah promptly knocked him off the cliff.

A short while later, he sat in the cave with a cup of ruka, grateful that the drink was hot. It was a keegrah brew, made from plants found on the side of the mountain, and although it was much lighter than rsakk ruka, it was savory. He'd turned down the fellow's offer of furs after seeing that the furs in the cave had not been used by anything but insects in a very long time.

As predicted, the keegrah rejected the jewel, though his face changed when he saw it. Perhaps it had given him some memories of home? That would be good for the story.

CHAPTER 3
An Agreement

My name is Oumid. That is, it is Oumid if you live in Tuklos and you are a grehti priest, or if you are my father Al-Medi. My real name you could not say it with your rsakk tongue, which is one of the reasons I chose it. If you were k'g'hrah you could say it.

Cough and then sneeze at the same time and that will be close enough.

If you cannot do it, then since you are rsakk and from Ak-Shamalim you may call me Oumid. The only time the priests use my other name is when they are going to ask me to do something no one else will do. They think it puts them in my favor. It doesn't, but it amuses me to hear them try to say it.

And you are the one who came up to my mountain in the cold, and sat in my cave in your nok form, your pale limbs shivering in the cold. You couldn't climb the whole way in your shape – you should have. It would be amusing to see you slip and scrape your way up on the rocks and ice. You would be a little more k'g'hrah, then. That is one of the ways we are trained.

I'm not afraid of you, no. Should I be?

Kill me then, and have done with it.

I thought so. I am of some value to you, or you would not have risked the cold.

You wear the grehti robes, but you don't talk like one, and you don't smell like one. I've seen grehti in the place where they let the caravans camp. The grehti don't like the shashigai, the storytellers. Yet you say you are both shashigai and grehti.

My history? Why is my story important?

I thought the important histories were all on tapestries. You're rsakk, why don't you just go read them? The tapestries hold all the stories of the people of the Mother. All the heroes are there already. The rsakk are the great holders of the history of Karn. Isn't that what you teach us at the child house? Isn't that what the mothers say?

Put your jewels away. What need have I of you? What need have you of my stories? I do not need help to tell my story. I do not need you. The sky alone is my partner.

You came here to call me, and you are grehti, so I have agreed to enter into your service. But you will not deceive me. You will gift me with things I do not want. Then you will ask me to do things others will not do. Know that I work for the grehti when they command me, and only to fight, or to kill demons. So do not send women or clothing to me. I have no need of fancy food. You may tell me to do tasks. You may look into my mind. I will answer your questions but I will not tell you stories.

The shashigai was frustrated, but he was thinking fast. The keegrah were quiet, private people, and he had been told that this one valued his privacy more than any trade item he might bring. It was clear from the man's anger that others had tried to get him to work or talk by bribing him with things most men would want. The shashigai needed to convince the keegrah to tell the story, but beyond the gem, he had nothing material to offer. He sighed to himself. It would be a lot of work – and a lot of bribes – to get the grehti to let go of their mercenary. But it would be worth it to get the story, if what the grehti Al-Medi had told him was true. He could not offer the keegrah a meeting with his former mentor; that might have worked but Al-Medi was in hiding. The deal would have to be made with keegrah currency. It had better work, because it was all he had left.

He made his offer.

I accept. Do you speak for all grehti? That if I tell you the stories you ask for, then all grehti will leave me alone? They will not come to my mountain and call me to do this thing or that thing? They will not call me to kill, to fight with the demons in the sky again?

This promise has been broken before. And already you have deceived me. You did not tell me that I would go away from the mountains to serve you. I want to go back to my sky, the one above Cnieren and the other k'g'hrah mountains. She will not come here among the trees. In the mountains it is cold, and there are places a k'g'hrah and his sky can go where no one would come. Each time I change my camp, they find me again. They call me away from my sky, and tell me that this is the last time. It never is. You say that you – that the grehti – will leave me alone? Can you assure me? They have said before that I should go and do what I want, and then they used mind power to find me.

My father? Al-Medi told you to find me? You should have said that before. Where is he?

Safe? What does that mean? Is Al-Medi dead? That is the only safety in Karn.

Not dead, but still safe?

The shashigai held up the only other thing he had that might convince the keegrah. He'd been told to use it only as a last resort. There were no other options. He held out the small bit of leather and wood, and the keegrah took it from him.

A shield! It is like the one Al-Medi has. If he gave it to you, then I will come with you. I will tell you my story. When I am finished, I will go away. The grehti will not follow or use mind powers to find me. This is what you have promised.

CHAPTER 4
It Was the Music

Her name was Marai, and she was beautiful.

It was the time of shapefinding. A grehti, one like you, climbed shivering all the way up to my mountain to bring me down for the celebration at Ak-Shamalim. Al-Medi had called for me – he was the most important grehti there. He was the leader, the elder of the school. He was also my father. When he called, I went. They have shapefinding at Tuklos, and those who are found rsakk go to Ak-Shamalim for the great celebration and to attend shapehouse. The shapefound there are sponsored by Esgeni jewelers or military leaders – even the grehti priests look to Ak-Shamalim for their initiates.

Tuklos is the biggest city in the badlands. It is very hot there, and many rsakk live there, but not other shapes, except the nethik slaves; there are some of those. The rsakk like the heat there because it is dry, not like the stuffy wet heat in the tirothi jungle. Also the sand is good for scale mites, those things that get under the scales and bite and bite and bite. You can just sweep them off if you're in nok shape, because there's nowhere for them to hide. But if you're rsakk, and you're in shape, then you can't get them with your claws, and you can't bite off your scales, and you can't burn them out because they just burrow deeper. If they burrow deep enough, then when you shift back, they stay under your skin and keep biting, little tiny bites that itch and itch and itch.

Why are you scratching?

Ak-Shamalim is the best shapehouse near Tuklos. The best ones are at Ak-Shamalim, and Ethkell, and Eileah (though that one is just for grehti). There's another one at Tollach. I went to that one after I was at Ak-Shamalim. I was born in Tuklos, and they thought I would be rsakk, but I was not. K'g'hrah can also go to the shapehouse at Esh, but they train many nethik there so it is not as good as Tollach.

My time in shapehouse? I thought you wanted to hear about Marai, the beautiful red one.

Very well. I will tell you about shapehouse before I tell you about Marai and her red hair.

I did not do well at Ak-Shamalim. I did not understand the drills. For some reason they want the k'g'hrah there to fly in groups instead of alone, as is their nature. But these k'g'hrah flew in a great group, like a cloud blocking the sky. At first, it was because I was awkward, but when I realized they meant to fly in front of me, I knocked them down on purpose.

The captain didn't like that, so for a while they did not let me do anything. It was Garad-grah who helped me; he explained to me that this was work, and I should tolerate it. He explained to the others that I needed the sky, but they were still wary of me for a while after that.

So for a time after that they made me do other jobs – things no one else wanted to do, like clean up after the shapesick k'g'hrah. For k'g'hrah, it is not good to be shapesick. The insides do not match the outsides, and many of them go mad, and that is what the barn is for, and I was to clean it after they beat themselves to death against the walls. The grehti would help some of them, but I don't know how they decided.

They also let me do things like clean up the fire pit – sometimes there was good meat there – if they had thrown in a tiroth. Tirothi are small and tender. But not many come to Ak-Shamalim. Nethik aren't good meat. Some say the horn and hooves taint it. No, never k'g'hrah. It is a grehti law – shape does not eat shape. Who would eat a shapesick k'g'hrah? You might become shapesick yourself.

The nethik live in the village below Ak-Shamalim. That is the other place I worked when I was there. They aren't allowed in Ak-Shamalim, the same way they aren't allowed in Tuklos and have to live outside the gates. I was the one sent to fetch them when they had to come with their wagons. Sometimes it was cloth or dyes or threads, but most days it was just water. I guess that way no one else had to become unclean by going into their village. In my eyes the others were just lazy – the nethik villages are small and close, and k'g'hrah and rsakk in shape are too large to fit through nethik streets. So you have to go in nok, and I guess they think that makes them the same as nethik; that is to say, weak. There's that order to the shapes, I know you know that – rsakk, who are our chosen leaders, then k'g'hrah who defend, and tirothi who are skilled with hands both in shape and in nok, and last there is nethik who have no hands when in shape, which means they serve the ones with hands.

But while I was doing those other things I was not learning k'g'hrah things, and I wanted to learn k'g'hrah things, so Al-Medi, who was in charge of Ak-Shamalim at that time, let me go from Ak-Shamalim and sent me to Tollach and there I learned more about how to be k'g'hrah – such as how to shift fast from nok to k'g'hrah without becoming ill. Every k'g'hrah becomes ill at first, but with practice it can be tolerated. I learned useful things about healing, and at Tollach they let me fly alone. They understood the k'g'hrah mind, which needs the sky alone.

38

Tollach it was where they discovered my real talents, and they thought at first that I was like a grehti, but then they tested me and found I could not mindspeak or hear. It was only the speritu I could hear, and only that kind of demon. I told them I could speak to the speritu but as everyone knows, the speritu are mad and cannot understand our words.

It was during a battle that they found this talent in me; the battle was against the demons. The speritu had gathered outside of Ethkell, where there are markets, and all manner of shapes live and trade there. There are fields outside of Ethkell where many caravans set camps, and word came to Tollach that the demons were attacking the caravans at night. The grehti thought this was not good for trade, so they called for rsakk and k'g'hrah soldiers.

This is the way I was taught to fight the demons: The rsakk breathe fire, and the demons are killed by it, or they flee from it – they flee from light too, which is why they were attacking at night. K'g'hrah carry rsakk to where the demons are, and drop them into the battle. This I was trained to do, and I did it better than anyone else because I could hear the demons.

It is said that speritu look like people in nok shape – just like people, but nearly invisible – one can see the outline of the body because it glows with a blue light. If you see it, and you do not have light or fire, then it is the last thing you see. It is said that with one touch the life of you goes out, and you are left cold and frozen. I have seen dead like that. Still, rsakk fire burns the speritu, and if they do not flee they are killed.

In my first battle I could not see them, but I could hear them. They cry and cry and cry. They cry for many things, but mostly hunger, and the life of a man is the only thing that feeds them. They come from the ground most of the time, but sometimes they just appear, even in the sky, so it was helpful that I could hear them crying before they came. I used to try calling to them. They did not listen and my battle mates began to think that I was mad. It was enough for them that I could hear the demons. Some of them liked me for that, and because of it, at first they wanted to fly with me. Others thought that somehow I was calling the demons, and so they did not want to fly with me.

The other thing they found out about me was that the speritu did not attack me. The sight of them is fearful to most people, and the demons seem to be drawn to fear, but I am not afraid of them. Perhaps that is why they do not attack me.

In that battle I was invisible to them unless I carried a rsakk warrior, and then they came toward me, but when I dropped the warrior, I became invisible to the demons again. Because of that I dropped a few warriors early. I thought that it was important that the demons did not kill me. Soon I learned to fly with rsakk who could burn the demons while we flew. After that the rsakk did not mind to fly with me.

The demons were why they called me to Ak-Shamalim. They called me from my camp above Cnieren. It was the time of shapefinding. The speritu had been seen near there, and they called for warriors with experience. I do not think of myself as a warrior, but for the grehti I do what I am told, and that is why I went there. Ak-Shamalim is the place where the shapefound who have wealth are sent. If you are not destined to be a soldier, you must pay a bribe to the grehti to go there. That means you have to be spoken for by one of the tribes of Tuklos – or you would need to be from a wealthy caravan. With so many important people there, the grehti did not want the celebration of the new shapefound to be spoiled by demons. So they sent for me, and others who had experience with speritu, and we went around Ak-Shamalim hunting for demons. We searched for days before the celebration, but we found none. But later there was one, the sperith that wanted Marai.

You sat up when I said that.

That is what you want to hear, isn't it? The story of Marai and her demon sister. I will tell you the story of Marai and her sperith and then you will leave me alone.

Marai was from one of the desert tribes – that is what the grehti said. She arrived at Ak-Shamalim after a desert shapefinding. Mother knows how they do those; their customs are different from the rsakk customs in the cities. She was beautiful – long red hair, the kind of body that gets the best bride price. If she did not call the fire of every man at the fire pit, then I am a tiroth and you are a melon.

I know rsakk beauty because I am from Tuklos. There are three good rsakk: the yellow, the green and the red. The brown often die, or should die, so we do not consider those. The yellow are the weakest and the smallest, usually unfit to be warriors – they often become traders. Most rsakk are green – they can call fire and are swift and fierce in battle.

I am reciting. This is how we learned it in the child house.

The red rsakk are the best rsakk. They are the most intelligent, the fiercest warriors, and their women are the best dancers. The red rsakk most often grow the extra claw which allows them advantage in battle. Although every child should hope to be a red, we should be glad when we are found rsakk.

The keegrah paused, and the shashigai allowed him to rest. The pause gave the shashigai time to think about his own shapefinding – how wonderful to be found rsakk, how his people had celebrated with songs and dance and gifts for him.

Training with the tribe of the shashigai had taught him different, but still there was something in him that rejoiced in the superiority of the rsakk to the other three shapes. Who else could breathe fire? Who else were strong in battle and had nothing to fear from the other shapes? Before the grehti came with their sacred teachings, the rsakk hunted the other shapes and put fear into their hearts.

For all that, the shashigai was a green rsakk. He was not trained as a warrior, but because of his wealth, he'd had many women attempt to draw his fire.

There were no stories about how the custom began, but every boy in the child house knew that if he were found rsakk, his power could be increased by the way a woman treated him. Rsakk mating was violent – the women bit and scratched and assaulted their mates. In response to this treatment, the man entered into a state wherein his internal gasses intensified, and his fire burned hotter and lasted longer. Most good warriors had at least one wife to draw his fire before a battle. The richest brought dancers to arouse the man even before he went to his wife's tent. Those were the most formidable; their behavior in battle struck terror into other shapes and rsakk alike.

The shashigai remembered his own encounter with a red woman, and that recollection occupied him until the keegrah was ready to continue.

Marai? She was a red rsakk. She had green in her too, but the red parts you could tell by the hair. For the red to be in the hair and less in the body is the very best for a woman because they don't need warrior's bodies.

She was not a dancer, but in a way, every rsakk woman is a dancer. They are taught to do the mating dance, to draw the man's fire so he will be strong in his battles. This is what they taught me to look for in a woman before they knew that I was k'g'hrah. I am happier as k'g'hrah. I need no woman to draw my fire.

But back then, at the great fire where they presented the shapefound, Marai danced. How could I help but be drawn to her? She was a small girl, and an angry one at that time – she stood before the fire with the other girls, the ones from Tuklos, and they scorned her. She had poor clothes and no one had paid her bride price, so she had no wrist bands. The other girls boasted whether theirs had gold or silver or fine ironwork, and this one and that one said how many jewels her husband had promised when she came from the shapehouse to his house or his tent. Marai had none, and the other girls said how she smelled like a nethik and her hair had no oils and how no one would pay her bride price. Even though she was from the desert, where they speak strange tongues, she understood what it meant when they laughed and pointed.

But then there was the dance. They call the dancers for the shapefound men – they want to show both the men and the women what it is to have the fire rise – that is part of what makes them able to breathe fire. The dancers are trained to make the fire rise in a man. Their steps mimic the rsakk hunt and the rsakk warriors as they fight. They dance to drums that raise the heartfire. There is a mating dance and a hunting dance. The mating dance movements are like mating. There is a part of it in shape and a part of it in nok. The most important dance is the fire dance.

The fire dance is both the hunt and mating. Step, watch, step look, step crouch – stalking, hunting, they dance in a circle, turning and looking and almost touching the men. Then they whirl, they crouch, they freeze – the drums fall silent, and then - pounce! They sweep by the men, brushing them with perfumed skirts and veils and leaning close – it would draw the fire of a nethik – if they had any.

The shashigai hid a yawn. It was the worst telling of the fire dance he'd ever heard. But several cups of ruka helped him tolerate it. It was important that the keegrah continue uninterrupted – only the Mother knew what might get him talking again if he stopped.

They don't have child houses in the desert, so Marai didn't know how to behave. She didn't know what to do, so she watched the dance. The other girls were from Tuklos; they were fidgeting and nudging each other and laughing at the dancers, because the dancers are very much like slaves. They are bred for the dance, and those of them who cannot dance serve the dancers. Their owners provide guards for them because the dance makes men wild with passion. The Tuklos girls were laughing because even though they are beautiful, the dancers would never have good husbands.

They were supposed to be watching to learn the parts that have to do with mating. But Marai didn't laugh. She was staring at the dancers. She looked like her own fire was rising. Her head was cocked listening to the drums; she was watching the dancers' every move, concentrating like a sarkoth about to pounce on its prey.

Then suddenly, before anyone knew what was happening, she got up and joined them. She was from the desert so she did not know that it was forbidden to dance with the dancers. Everyone knew, but no one stopped her.

The dancers are trained not to stop – that would be bad for the fire. So they didn't stop. The priests were shocked (or maybe entranced), and one went to stop her but the others held him back.

It was as if she was born to the dance. The rag she had tied her hair with fell off, her hair swept out so she was fire against the flames – no one could be looking at her clothes, not with that red hair, not with those slow, tantalizing steps, weaving in and out with the dancers. I know she was not perfumed – she could not have afforded it – but when she swept close to the men, I saw their fire rise. If I had fire, mine would have risen. I could not help but watch. The dancers have men with them, whose job it is to guard them and to keep the other men from mating with them as they dance. When men with their eyes on Marai rose from their places, the men who were guarding the dancers pushed them back as if Marai was one of the dancers. But the guards had their eyes on her too. My eyes were on her too, and although my fire did not rise, I felt other things which I had not felt before. I wanted her. It was not good, I know that now.

That was how I came to do work for the grehti that I did not wish to do and how finally they gave me a task from which I wished to escape, and the end of all of it is why I am here, and why you had to call me by my chosen name, which is not Oumid. Oumid is a rsakk name. Oumid cannot fly. Oumid is weak for the company of Marai.

But Oumid will tell you the story, if you give Kgh'jsh some time to rest. The telling of stories without pause is for the shashigai, and Kgh'jsh is not shashigai. He needs something to eat.

The storyteller smiled. Kgh'jsh wanted to tell his story, for all it made him angry and recalcitrant.

While he was eating Kgh'jsh said nothing, and when he was finished eating he said nothing. Instead he sat in the shashigai's caravan wagon and fingered his flute. Was he lost in memory? Had sadness changed his mind? The caravan had been moving since Kgh'jsh had started his story. The shashigai's nethik were among the fastest. By the time he stopped, they were a fair distance from the mountains. It did seem that the further they moved from the mountains, the more preoccupied the keegrah had become. But the shashigai had also been told that Kgh'jsh liked stories.

Perhaps hearing a bit of story would help.

When the caravan stopped and camped, meat was hunted and eaten and some of it was cooked for those who wanted it, and after the meal ruka was passed around the fire. Oumid-Kgh'jsh sat with his cup of ruka, staring into space. He seemed as strange as the stories had made him out to be. He did not join the men laughing and talking; he stayed in the shashigai's wagon.

The shashigai decided to see what effect another story would have on the keegrah.

It was a ritual storytelling – ruka had been distributed, and the fire built up high. The caravan was still moving through nethik territory, so the trees loomed around the listeners and the teller. The wagons were set in a semi-circle at the edge of the clearing, providing protection from whatever predators were foolish enough to take on humans. The trees were tall, close, old trees – the lowest branches were far above the heads of the group, and there was only a limited view of the sky. The listeners sat close to the fire – it was in woods such as these that demons could come and silently steal away the life of anyone who strayed too far from the light. The fire would be kept long after the stories ended, and guards would be on alert for any sign of the speritu. The light and the ruka diminished thoughts of demons, and the men were eager for the added distraction of the shashigai's storytelling.

The shashigai began his story.

"This is the story of the first shapefinding, in which the wildness of the shapes was found to be sacred to the Mother, who blessed and named them."

Zev stole a glance at Kgh'jsh and smiled to himself. The lad wasn't sitting up but he had stopped playing with his flute. A good start.

"In the early days of Karn there was no shapefinding, no knowledge of the Mother and no grehti to guide men to their shapes. There was chaos because the shapes did not recognize each other. There were no rules to guide the people: men in shape hunted the nok who did not know how to change, and nok men hunted the shapes for their meat.

"In those days there was a nok man named Hsora the Strong. He was the strongest man in his tribe, and they made him the leader. At certain times, he watched his people become beasts and animals and hunt people from other tribes in their shapes, and people from other tribes hunted his people in their shapes. Even within his tribe people would become animals and hunt the people who had been their companions the day before. The only thing they knew for certain was that the change happened at skydark, when both moons have gone to rest with the Mother before beginning their journey through the sky again.

The killings made Hsora sad. Each day there were fewer and fewer people, and there was no way to defend against someone who was nok one day but might be a beast the next day. He set off on a quest of wisdom, to see if this was the way of the whole world, or if there was some better way that his people might survive. His people, weary of fighting, agreed to wait for his return to see if something could be done.

"As he traveled into the hills and mountains, Hsora thought that if he went to a different kind of place, that he would find a different kind of people. He was right. His intent was to travel over the mountains, but once he reached them, he came to a place which was by its people called Eileah.

"Eileah was marked as a sacred place by the presence of a circle of stones standing at the edge of a cliff. Near the circle, which was larger than a house but smaller than a village, there was a village. In that village lived a group of people who seemed to be at peace. There were people in the shapes of animals and people in nok shape, and they did not attack each other.

"These people had learned that there were four shapes held sacred by the Mother, and they cultivated those shapes by helping the people control the change. This they did by touching the mind of a man while he was in nok shape, so that he could find his shape and also have control over when he changed.

"They were able to touch the mind of Hsora the Strong, and he changed into an animal! His shape was that of a rsakk, and Hsora was surprised to find that he could talk and think and do all of the things that a man could do. The people at Eileah explained to him that there was a part of a man's mind that could be altered so that when he shifted, so that he retained the ability to think and act like a man.

"Of course, now that he understood the shift, Hsora was happy to have found these men. He asked if one of them would come back to his village and help his people. The people at Eileah agreed to send one of their elders, and the elder they sent was Abadran-rsakk.

51

"When Hsora and Abadran returned to the village they discovered that the people had not waited; instead they had declared war on another tribe, and Hsora's people were fighting the other tribe as well as each other, because they did not know who would take a shape and kill someone.

"Hsora tried to talk to the people to tell them that he had brought them hope, but neither his tribe nor the other tribe would listen, and they continued to attack and kill each other.

"Hsora and Abadran had to hide in the woods because when the people saw Abadran, they wanted to kill him before he could become an animal and attack them. So Hsora and Abadran went into the woods and hid and waited for skydark, which was the time that people would become animals.

"At skydark, the people were running back and forth in panic, because even in the safety of their houses, people were changing into animals. There were nethik stabbing people with their horns, rsakk burning people and houses and tirothi climbing into the trees and jumping on people to bite them with poison fangs.

"But Hsora came out and Abadran was with him, and they stood in the middle of the village. Hsora shouted that they should look at him. Some of the people did, and when they did, he changed into his shape and showed them his fire, but the fire was too strong and a house was burned.

"This was bad because it was not Hsora's house, but it was good because the people looked at the fire, and when they did they saw Hsora change from an animal back into a man. They crowded around him and Abadran, and begged for safety.

"So Abadran and Hsora breathed fire on any animals who tried to harm the people, and the night passed with no one else in Hsora's village killed.

"Hsora ordered that everyone in his village be helped by the people from Eileah. It was found that each shape best helped its own. Rsakk for rsakk, k'g'hrah for k'g'hrah, tiroth for tiroth, and nethik for nethik. This is why there are four elder grehti at each shapefinding. The first elder shapefinder was grehti Abadran, of the rsakk race, the second was grehti Sean of the k'g'hrah. After them came grehti Sh'tai of the tirothi and grehti Kilani of the nethik. These were sent from Eileah to help Hsora's people learn their shapes.

"These are the four sacred shapes that the Mother has ordained for Karn; the rsakk who run swiftly and breathe fire, the k'g'hrah, the tirothi who climb in the trees and have poison fangs, and the nethik who are like taralk but can change back into men.

"And from that time on the shapefinding was conducted at every village at each skydark which is when the shape magic is strongest.

Zev stole a glance at the keegrah, who was by now sitting up and watching. The others in the listening group were waving their hands in gestures of appreciation but the keegrah just sat looking at Zev. The shashigai smiled to himself. He'd left out part of the story on purpose; he hoped it would work. Sure enough, later, in the shashigai's wagon, the keegrah confronted him, eager to fill in the left out part of the story.

CHAPTER 5
Why the K'g'hrah Fly

You did not speak of the k'g'hrah, or say why they fly. That is an important part of the story of shape changing. The k'g'hrah fly because the world is a heavy place. Even the air can be felt to lean upon the k'g'hrah, unless there is a wind. If there is a wind, I must fly.

There is room in the sky. I am not smothered by trees and houses and other people. In the air I am not bothered by the awful noises that people make. The air understands wings, it lifts them. It lifts me. Other than food, this is all I need.

The rsakk have fire. The nethik have the forest and their lands. The tirothi have – well, they have a lot of pretty shiny things. K'g'hrah – I – have the sky. Some k'g'hrah settle for wives. I will not settle for less than the sky.

The wind holds me while I fly. The wind speaks to me; it is the voice of the sky. If I speak to you of flying I might not find the words for things only a k'g'hrah can know.

But since you ask, I will try. Flying is a story that does not hurt to tell.

The best places to fly are the mountains with cliffs and other high places. Trees are not a good place to fly; first because if I land among them it will be hard to get up high again, and second because it is hard to hold to the top branches with k'g'hrah feet.

From the cliffs I can find the warm rising winds that lift me and mean that I do not have to move my wings much. There are currents in the air on which I can drift for hours, resting on the winds and going where they take me. There are those currents even in the mountains. Sometimes if it is the right kind of wind I can rest in one place while the wind rocks me. It is like nothing on the ground – there is no bed softer than the sky!

Learning to fly was hard work. Both at Ak-Shamalim and at Tollach there were drills every day. At Ak-Shamalim the drills were shorter because of the heat of the days. If they made me fly during the hot times I drank cartfuls of water. At Tollach the drills were from first light to starlight; then sleep and then fly again. There was water in the mountains if I became thirsty. In the mornings there was no formation because I was required to hunt for first meal. But after that there was flying in formation for many hours, and even if there were updrafts I had to move my wings. This was to make the muscles strong. After formation there was free time but only a short time of it was allowed to be on the ground. After free time there was more formation, and more free time in the air and then more formations. There was ruka at the end of the day, which was good because by then I groaned with pain. I do not like formations because most times I am not at the front, and then I cannot see my sky, and I have to think hard to remember that I am not allowed to knock down the k'g'hrah in front of me.

When we became strong enough, formations were done while carrying people, at first in nok shape, and then later shivering rsakk. At Tollach the rsakk did not like the cold, but it was necessary for the warriors to learn to carry them, and Tollach is one of the important shapehouses, so the rsakk had to come there.

The free times were good, although at first I got in trouble because I could not tell time. I came back late from free times and was reprimanded by the training captain. I had to learn the sun all over again because the rising and mid day and setting of it were different. I had to learn the stars all over too because they are different in Tollach. The moons were the same but in different places in the sky.

During the free times I could rest on the arms of the sky and listen to the wind. It is a different sound when I am flying; some of the time it is a whisper, and sometimes it is a rushing sound. Perhaps like a sandstorm? That is a kind of wind I do not like because it is hard to fly. Sand gets under my feathers and in my mouth and eyes. But at Tollach there was no sand so I could spend all my free time with my sky.

Flying is different from running because to change direction all that is required is a shift of the wings. When running I have to stop and turn and then start running in the new direction. Flying does not jar my bones. K'g'hrah bones are lighter unless I am in nok shape. Nok feels very heavy after flying. That is why k'g'hrah spend free times flying or in camp. Camps are very high up and from there it is easy to shift and fly if I feel too heavy.

If I am feeling heavy I can get better when the sky rocks me. If I hold my wings the right way it will happen, but that is a thing that takes practice. It is a peaceful feeling. The best times are when the sun is warm and the air is cold. That makes the right comfort. If the air is warm already then the sun feels hot. If there is no sun there is danger of rain. Rain is not good for k'g'hrah feathers and fur. It makes it hard to fly.

I do not know how to describe flying except that it is not as heavy as walking.

When they sent me to Tollach I had already learned to shift, so when they left me at the bottom of the cliff, I just flew up after them. It was the first test, and it was hard because the cliffs are higher than at Ak-Shamalim. When I cleared the last ledge, then it was that I knew how much I loved the sky. It was blue and cold and wind as far as I could fly. It was as beautiful as some find rsakk women.

At Tollach the grehti live in a stone house, not a compound. There are four grehti and sometimes others there; one for each shape and others who come and go. Tollach is good for nethik and for k'g'hrah, but the rsakk only go there when they are ordered to do so, and few tirothi go there at all; it is too cold for them and they always get sick.

I was supposed to report to the training leader, but I felt the air in my wings and in my chest and it was cold and delicious. Everywhere above me was blue and everywhere below me was green and grey; those were new colors to me. There were meadows with taralk just standing in them, not hiding under the sand like the worms in the badlands.

The sky went on forever, and I knew that I was home. I could not help myself. I flew long and far and they sent out a k'g'hrah captain after me. He told me to come back but I thought that he was disturbing me. How was I to know what he was saying? No one had taught me k'g'hrah speak. He went back when I did not answer, and finally they sent a grehti who reached into my mind. I felt the touch; it was like an arrow flew into my head. I clapped my hands to my ears. Then I realized he had done something else.

I fell.

He caught me, of course. But I was shapesick for a time after that, and they confined me to the barns. They call them the healing barns, but all I ever saw there were k'g'hrah who could not shift, half nok and half k'g'hrah, and in terrible pain. Many would beat themselves to death against the walls, just like at Ak-Shamalim. I hid in one of the stalls the whole time I was there. The place smelled of stale k'g'hrah blood and death. No one ever came in; there was food, but it was put in through a small hole at the bottom of the door. I tried to leave, but when I went outside there was a guard who told me I had to stay inside, so I went back in until they called me to come out.

When I got out of the healing barns I joined the other k'g'hrah students in the barracks; by then they were doing formations. I learned them fast; it went well for me because the formations were all in patterns, and patterns are easy for me. I do not say that I liked them, but at Tollach anyone who does not fly in the formations is told to leave.

There were many k'g'hrah at Tollach; perhaps the same amount as a village; not a large one, like Ak-Shamalim, but like the ones on the edge of the forest. I found out quickly that they were like me, in need of being alone, and I learned about the camps that they made to go and have privacy. These camps were already set up, with a fire pit and sometimes even a cloth made of leaves to cover the entrance. This was because there are some seasons when the cold is very cold even for a k'g'hrah. Any k'g'hrah could use any camp so long as it was not occupied. I could tell by sight most of the time and by smell at other times, when a k'g'hrah was in his camp, and then I would fly until I found another.

If I did not say before, I will say now that the best part of Tollach was the sky – they let me fly again almost immediately after I returned from the healing barns. They declared that I had learned my lesson. It was true. I did not go far from Tollach unless they ordered me. There were enough high places there, and the blue sky was with me.

When I flew at Tollach, I could feel it much more than at Ak-Shamalim – the sky spoke to me, held me, lifted me up. The air was cold and friendly. How can I describe it? It is k'g'hrah mind to understand the sky. The k'g'hrah at Tollach were the same as me. They did have different thoughts about other things, but they understood the sky. Even the women there had k'g'hrah mind. They did not squabble over perfumes and oils and bangles. They flew formation (but not in the same one as the men), they mated and they cooked for the men.

I was very surprised when I was told I did not have to choose a wife. It was expected at Ak-Shamalim, even though I was k'g'hrah. This was because my father was rsakk. But the k'g'hrah at Tollach mated with who they wanted, and the women all lived together and cooked for the men who could not hunt, and for the children. They told me that this was the way they lived in the k'g'hrah villages too, and the k'g'hrah villages are in the mountains, most of them, and the k'g'hrah there do stonework and other things of that nature. They did not have a Tapestry Master, although they did have storytellers. They have one in each village, and he tells the stories of the village. They do not wander like the shashigai. They had one for Tollach, but he only told stories of fighting and battles. I could not learn from him the nature of the sky.

That is what I wanted most to learn, the nature of the sky. That is one reason I was glad to return to Ak-Shamalim after I was at Tollach. I learned to fly at Ak-Shamalim, and for all that they are fierce warriors, the k'g'hrah there were kind. Some of them had been at Ak-Shamalim all their lives. Some had been born there or at Tuklos, and they did not mind the heat as much.

At Tollach they shoved me off the cliff. At Ak-Shamalim, they carried me the same way they carry the rsakk warriors. That made my arms strong. Tirothi and nethik are rare inside the walls of Tuklos, so it was assumed that I would fly like k'g'hrah or be carried as rsakk.

When I was a young boy, I was big and strong, so they chose me even before the mothers started talking about who would find what shape. Instead of playing the worm hunting games with the boys, I was carried to Ak-Shamalim, first alone, and then in a formation, and finally with weapons. The weapons were made of wood because it is awkward to fly with such things and we dropped them at first.

How should I describe it? At Ak-Shamalim one does not wait until after shapefinding to fly. As a boy, maybe ten summers, I was made to stand with my arms outstretched. There were warriors in the fields with us, and this was after many long nights of torture and pain. The warrior said that today we would learn what it was to be a warrior.

On a skydark they started the training, by standing all the boys in a line, and I was made to hold my arms out like that, like the warriors do when they are carried. But they did not carry us at that time. Instead they hung sacks of stones on each arm, and the boys who cried were sent away. That was good, because it got worse. To me the stones weighing down my arms were a curious sensation; sometimes I imagined I was a nethik pulling a cart of iron ore to the k'g'hrahworks, or pulling a cart of unfinished swords to the gates of Tuklos. Sometimes I would flex my shoulders to see if I could raise the sacks after I had tired. I stood that way through the night and in the darkness, and in the morning I was allowed to drop the stones, but right after that they came with a sack of sand and hit me on my back. I thought it was a game, and that the object was to remain standing. But for this game they did not send anyone away if they fell. I fell two or three times. Next they made me stand even longer with the sacks of stones and finally they made me stand with the stones while they hit me with the sack.

Each morning they came the sacks of sand were heavier. Sometimes I would spend the day in pain from it, but we still had to come back and stand again the next night.

They also taught me to roll in the sand; I was made to jump from high rocks and roll so that I did not get hurt when I fell. That game was unpleasant since it meant that I would have sand in my clothes and in my hair. This was to train for when the k'g'hrah would drop me into a battle, because at that time they thought I would be a rsakk.

After many nights of standing and many days of pain there came a time when they could hit me with a full sack of sand, a sack of stones on each arm and I did not fall. Then I went to the line with the other boys and they said that I would be a warrior. I stood as they told me, and I watched as each boy ahead of me walked to a boulder and stood on it. Then there was a strong wind, and part of the test was to stand in our places. Any who did not were sent back to the training.

The wind was from the wings of a k'g'hrah!

I had seen them training – there were not as many at Tuklos as there were at Ak-Shamalim, but they trained just outside the gates, and I watched them. That was how I knew that the boy standing on the rock was going to be picked up by a k'g'hrah.

This was the meaning of the training – to make my shoulders strong so that the k'g'hrah could carry me, and to make me strong enough to stand while the k'g'hrah picked me up – it felt just like a sack of sand was hitting me! The games were training for a k'g'hrah to pick me up, just like the warriors.

The k'g'hrah came quickly – there were four, and each one picked up a boy and carried him to a place further away. They dropped them there, and that part was not getting hurt when I was dropped, and I did not because I remembered my training and rolled in the sand.

The one who picked me up was Yaras, who was the son of Garad who was the leader of the k'g'hrah at Ak-Shamalim. He lifted me into the sky and at first I felt as though I would fall, but then I felt lighter and lighter. The wind rushed past us, and I could hear the song of the sky. It was very blue, the sky that day. I did not feel my arms aching from the grip of his claws. I only felt the blue of the sky wrap itself around me. The voice of the sky spoke to me to tell me that I was not alone; that there would be joy in the vast empty blue.

That first day Yaras only carried me short distances. But each day we flew higher and longer, and each time the sky welcomed me and I grew more familiar with her. Finally we were ready to fly to Ak-Shamalim.

The other boys gritted their teeth and made bets about who would squirm and be dropped by his k'g'hrah. I did not make any bets because it was inevitable that people would be dropped.

I was not dropped. Yaras brought me back and forth to Ak-Shamalim for many days, and then some boys went to stay in the caves while others went to stay at Ak-Shamalim. The boys in the caves were going to learn to hunt the worms that lived there; they were going to be trained to be hunters and provide meat for Tuklos and its merchants and warriors.

Those of us who went to Ak-Shamalim were going to be warriors. Even though we were still in the child house, they said that we should learn things from the warriors who were being trained in the camp at Ak-Shamalim. At first all we learned was to pick up dung for the carts that went to the nethik villages. We learned how to haul water and how to sweep out the tents. Some of the boys grumbled about this and went back to Tuklos. But Ak-Shamalim was much smaller than Tuklos. It was quiet there, so I did not complain because I wanted to stay.

I met Al-Medi because once the other boys, the ones who did not like it, had gone home, I started to get in trouble. This was because my littermate Tariq left. Until then he was with me all the time, and at that time he was my friend. He swore that he would stay with me all the time and explain things to me. He said that he should do that because I was simple and that without him I would get in trouble.

He started explaining things to me in the child house; that was to keep me from getting into trouble. It was him that explained to me that when the mothers sent us to market, we should steal what they wanted us to get and use the things they gave us for trading to get things for ourselves. At first I did not understand this but he explained that the mothers did not have enough trades for goods and treats, and so since the treats were more carefully guarded, we should buy those and steal things like tools and cloth. He showed me which things to steal and also helped me by distracting the merchants. Later the mothers and the merchants changed their minds about that. It was after I asked mother Dimah to give us a list of things that could be stolen instead of traded. I was having a hard time keeping the items sorted in my head, and Tariq was frustrated with me. After that the mothers sent me with a list of items only to trade, which was good because one list is easier to remember. They sent me with someone else, and Tariq did not go at all; in fact for a time after that he was at the healing tents. I only asked him once what happened because when I did he knocked me down and was angry.

But he was among those chosen to go to Ak-Shamalim; he boasted to the girls that he would come back as a warrior and that he would buy wives even before he was shapefound. Tariq said that sweeping out tents was nethik work. After we had been cleaning tents for a while he said that he was worried about the girls and went back to Tuklos.

After that I started to get into trouble.

It was because I had not learned how to understand words. Tariq used to tell me what people meant by what they said; he said there were always two meanings. For example, if a shopkeeper said, don't touch that, usually he meant "Don't touch that while I am watching," and some of them meant don't touch that at all, and Tariq was able to tell which ones meant which things.

At Ak-Shamalim it was the same. There were times when they told us to get water from the nethik carts, and Tariq said they meant for us to tip over the water so that the nethik would go and get fresh water. This made some sense, but it did not make sense for us to do it when they were not looking. If we did it when they were not looking they would not understand to get more water.

So after Tariq left I had to guess which times they meant to tip the water, and I also thought that it would be kinder to do it in front of them. After that the guards hit my head and beat me and took me to Al-Medi. I explained to him that I had to guess which things people meant, and he listened to me and after a time he laughed. No one else had laughed. All of them had yelled at me and hit me and said that I was wasting water.

But Al-Medi asked me my name, and I told him (it was different back then), and he told me that if I had a question about something someone said, that I should tell him, and he would help me to understand what they meant. But he also told me something that was very helpful, and that is that if someone says something with words and I do not understand the second meaning, the person who spoke must explain the second meaning to me or be at fault if I do not understand. That was a great relief to me, and it worked very well. I did not get into very much trouble at all after that.

I also used to talk to Al-Medi about things that I heard while sweeping out the tents. It seemed as if I was invisible to the men there. They would talk about things I did not understand. I would talk to Al-Medi about those things and that made him happy, though sometimes the things I repeated made him angry.

One of the things that made him angry was hearing that the men made me stay with the nethik boys and do the things the nethik boys were doing. He said that I should be with the boys from Tuklos, and that part of the problem was that I did not have a proper rsakk name. That was true. So he gave me the name Oumid, which is a rsakk name, and after some time everyone knew who I was and they knew that I was not a nethik boy. That was good because the boys from the nethik village got hit a lot more than the ones from Tuklos, and I did not like being hit.

I did well at Ak-Shamalim when I was apprenticed there. But it was only for two summers; after that I had to go back to Tuklos because they wanted to see if I would make a good Esgeni.

I did not make a good Esgeni; I was supposed to be there for two summers and they sent me back after only one. Then I had to stay in the child house until my shapefinding, and it was boring because I had already learned how to do all of the things they do in the child house. I was big even when I was there with my littermates; when I went back everyone else was ten summers or less. I went with them as the mothers asked, but the children would not play with me or allow me to join in hunting rockrats and baby worms. Tariq came to see me a few times; he did well in the houses of the Esgeni. They liked him and even let him trade with the tirothi men who came to trade findings for jewels and for knives and swords. That is what the Esgeni do: they hit the jewels with hammers and stones and make them shine; they also make the knives and swords sharp and shiny. They are very wealthy; I was surprised that they did not speak for Tariq at shapefinding; but I was glad that he went to Ak-Shamalim because it meant that I would know someone there.

But then I failed my military training at Ak-Shamalim because I loved the sky more, and Al-Medi sent me to Tollach. When I went to Tollach I did not return to Ak-Shamalim until Al-Medi called for me, and that was after I was finished training at Tollach, and after I saw what happened at Merinell.

CHAPTER 6
A Place to Go

This part of the story really isn't about what happened at Merinell because by the time I got there it was too late to do anything. It's just that Merinell came before Ak-Shamalim, and many more people died at Merinell. I was finished my training at Tollach by that time, but I had nowhere to go because no one had spoken for me at Tuklos, and at Tollach I did not learn the things a k'g'hrah should know to make a living. There was a grehti at Tollach named Teren, and it was his job to talk to people like me about where we should go after our training was complete. The warriors went wherever they were spoken for, but nobody spoke for me. So it was Teren's work to find a place for me to go.

"Oumid," he said, "You would make a good farmer."

"But I am not a nethik."

"There are k'g'hrah farmers to the west and south of here. You would be comfortable."

"What kind of towns are there?"

"They are small towns and all kinds of people are there. You would like it because they have all the shapes, not just one or two. It would be interesting."

"Is the sky there?"

He did not understand that. He did not understand that I have to be with the wind and in the sky. I thought surely he would understand that since he was a k'g'hrah. But he was not in the military and he was a grehti, so he did not shift very often, except during the shapefindings and if he had to go to Eileah or Ethkell. He preferred to be in his hut being taken care of by his wife. There are k'g'hrah like that and they are not shapesick. So I think that he did not understand that I needed to be in the sky.

I went to the villages where the farms were; one of them was Merinell. It is not there any longer; no one wanted to go back even though the land was good for farming. They think the demons are still there.

When I went there to see about joining one of the farms, it was a nice place. It was not as quiet as some of the farm villages south of the forbidden forest. It was a wealthy village because they supplied things to Ethkell. The farms around the forbidden forest bear some of the best crops of all kinds: grains and vegetable and fruit. Because the farms were good the cattle were good; they had taralk the size of nethik! Taralk meat is much more tender than nethik meat and it does not have that sour taste that sometimes makes your food come back up after you eat it.

I went to three farms at Merinell. One was a grain farm and I could not stay there because something from the grain plants made me sneeze unless I was in shape. There was no use for a k'g'hrah in shape on a grain farm, so I went to the next one, which was a vegetable farm.

At the vegetable farm they had rows and rows of plants and the farmers went out each day to make sure there were no bugs or rodents and to pray for rain. The grehti helped them with this, and when the farmers were not picking bugs or digging out the rodents they made tools and repaired tools and chopped wood. I worked with them for one day and they said that I could come there after I finished at Tollach. I think they found me useful because I dug out some rodents that no one else could find. I could hear them moving and scratching in their burrows when no one else could hear them. They said I could stay there, but Teren said to visit all the farms, so I went to the next one.

The last farm at Merinell was a taralk farm, and because they were using grain plants to feed the taralk I could not stay there either.

There were some other farms south of the forbidden forest that I went to see. I did not go to see the ones north of Ethkell because those were too close to the tirothi jungle, which meant that it was hot and wet, and I already knew that I would not like that.

I liked the vegetable farm at Merinell best because they had some open fields and it meant that I would be able to fly. The sad thing was that they told me that after the picking and digging and praying and making and fixing tools was done, usually it was time to sleep. During the cold moons there would be more time to do what I wanted to do, but during the cold moons many times the skies are cloudy and the light does not last very long, so it is not good for flying.

Teren was happy that I had found a place; they did not want me to stay at Tollach because I could not earn my keep there. They sent me on some errands and gave me some things to do, but I could not keep in the formation, and when we did go to fight demons I sometimes dropped my rsakk too early so that many of them did not want to fly with me. I did not think it was too early since I could hear the demons coming, but they said it was not good for formation or for training.

Those battles were easy; most times we would go and there were no more than a handful of demons. But sometimes it took more than one rsakk to kill them.

While I was waiting to go to Merinell I went from Tollach on some errands to Ethkell and to Eileah. At Eileah they were very interested in me and tested me, but the outcome was the same as it had been at Tollach; I was not able to become a grehti. I was surprised to find that they had captive demons at Eileah. They did not have many – perhaps three. The grehti were studying them so they did not kill them.

It was while I was waiting for the people at the farm to speak for me to Teren when a call came from Merinell for help because the speritu were attacking them.

Three k'g'hrah had set out from Merinell to come to Esh and Ethkell and Tollach. Ethkell is a trade town but they have k'g'hrah warriors there. Esh is the k'g'hrah shapehouse just north of Eileah; there they have k'g'hrah and tirothi and nethik warriors. Tollach is where the k'g'hrah that do not go to Esh go for shapehouse. Those were the places closest to Merinell, and they sent to all three places because there were so many speritu.

At that time the head of the Tollach warriors was a k'g'hrah named Edrik; when the call came he did not believe that so many k'g'hrah needed to go. We had two squads of rsakk because it was the warm season, and one of tirothi for the same reason. When he heard that k'g'hrah messengers had been sent to Ethkell and to Esh as well as to Tollach, Edrik said that only one hand of men would go. The tirothi did not go because the tirothi cannot fight speritu. The hand of men had been gone only a short while when a patrol came back and reported that a big fire was burning in the area where Merinell should be. It was a big fire they set to frighten the speritu, but by then there was a lot of chaos and the speritu were in the air and on the ground and under the ground as well. This we heard from the k'g'hrah who came to call for help.

He told Edrik that there were many, many speritu, more than anyone had seen; they were killing all the people and there were still more to attack the warriors when they came. He said that there were no k'g'hrah come from Esh or from Ethkell. Edrik sent the rest of the rsakk and I went too because he said everyone should go. By the time I got there it was too late; much of the k'g'hrah squad was dead, and some of the rsakk, except the ones that had run toward Ethkell.

The demons had fed and were satisfied; they were not defeated; I think they just went away.

Edrik came down to see and told us that we should look for survivors to tell what had happened. I found one girl who ran away from me and then I could not find her. But also there was a woman found in one of the huts; she was as if dead but her body was warm, so they brought her out. When she awakened she asked to go to Ethkell. All of us in my squad went to take her to Ethkell. We found out there that they had not had any alarm or warning. The messenger sent to warn Ethkell had not reached the city, and the messenger sent to Esh had not reached that shapehouse. We found them later: they were both dead at Merinell, frozen between nok and k'g'hrah, not shapesick, but frozen dead as they shifted by the touch of the demons.

So then I could not go to Merinell, because the people who worked on the farm were gone. Teren was upset when I asked and said I should do what I wanted, so I went into the mountains near Cnieren and lived there until Al-Medi called me to tell me he needed me. I went down to Cnieren once in a while to trade for things like leather bags and cloth. I stayed there until Al-Medi sent a grehti to climb up to my camp and ask me to go to Ak-Shamalim.

It was in the camp at Cnieren that the sky became my partner. There was no one there but me; they have the same custom in Cnieren, that if it seems that someone is in a camp, the k'g'hrah who finds it will find another camp to use.

I did not move a lot because I was not disturbed while I was in those camps. One time I went down to Cnieren and they had traders from far away; one of them was selling musical instruments. None of the Cnieren k'g'hrah wanted them because they had their own instruments made of wood, but the trader had a flute made of a very hard wood that sounded to me like the voices I heard in the wind. He was a tirothi trader and he had made the flute himself. It was carved with very intricate designs that reminded me of rsakk, so I thought that I would trade for it. He was very happy to trade it with me when he saw the jewels I had brought with me from Ak-Shamalim. He talked to me a long time and gave me the whistle made of bone, and showed me how it was made so that if I lost mine, I might make another.

He showed me how to make the flute talk, and to my delight it did sound like the sky voices. He also sold me the cloth for the clothes I wear. It was dyed with nethik dye, and no one wanted it because the color was wrong; but it was the color of the sky so I asked for it.

At the end of our trade he said I should give him a jewel for each thing that he had given me, including the instructions on how to use the flute. But Al-Medi told me that one jewel was worth a cart full of trades, and I only had an armful. But since there was nothing else I wanted I gave him a jewel.

He told me that he had some things that were better, that I might want; he said that he would bring those things to my camp and I told him no, but I think he followed me. One day I came back from flying and I found my things scattered all around. The cloth was torn and everything else was broken. I had some things to trade in a pack and that was gone, but those were only carvings I made on days when there was too much rain to fly.

My jewels were in a pouch around my neck because Al-Medi told me I should always carry them, even if I was in shape, and I liked to have them because they reminded me of him. The flute was gone but the bone whistle was not because that was on the string too.

When I came down from my camp to find the trader I found out that there were some men looking for him the same as me. This was because they had found some things missing, not from their camps, but from the town. They asked me to go down with them because they thought he had gone down the trail to the nethik camp. I went with them but we did not find him.

The nethik were looking for him too because he had taken some cloth meant for grehti robes – the cloth was blue, and I wondered if it was like my cloth. But my cloth could not be used for a robe because it was torn.

I got the flute back later because the trader got hurt. They found him in the forest and he got hurt and died and the men who found him found all the things he had taken from Cnieren and my flute was there. They gave me back the jewel, and the next day they gave me some good nethik porridge to eat, made from tirothi brains, which is the best meat next to Merinell taralk.

After that no one bothered me; I could sit in my camp in nok or in shape, and no one came. The sky with clouds is beautiful except when it rains, and then it is not good to be outside because it is hard to fly. And I could play my flute and talk to the sky.

There is something special about the sky at Cnieren. Something special, something blue, that calls me. That is k'g'hrah mind, and it is why most of the camps there can only be accessed by those who can fly.

From those camps, those cliffs, I can leap over the edge and catch the wind just right; it will not only carry me, but it will hold my wings open to catch more wind, and then it is rest and release; my feet can forget the hard stones I walked on in the morning, and I forget the weight holding me down when I am in nok shape.

All through the cold season I was there; Merinell happened in the planting season, and then there was a time of confusion and I could not ask any questions of Teren or anyone else. But after many things happened I was able to ask, and then they said I should do what I wanted. The many things were that k'g'hrah came from other places to stay at the shape house. They were already trained, but now they were going to live there so that there would be men with experience there and not just students. The towns around the forbidden forest were going to send food and supplies for these men and in exchange for that the men would go to the towns if there was an alarm about speritu.

Through the traders I heard that there was another speritu attack. This time they came outside of Ethkell. They were met by warriors, from rsakk and k'g'hrah, and even tirothi and nethik tribes. There were grehti with spells and lights. But the ones who told the stories of that day spoke in quiet voices and asked for the Mother's blessing. They said that the great army of rsakk and k'g'hrah that had assembled at Ethkell had been defeated. The speritu came forth in great numbers and even the fires and lights were not enough. There were many dead, and many wounded who died later from a coldness that could not be healed with furs or with fire.

I think they did not call me because I was in my camp. K'g'hrah from Cnieren were called and some did not return, but those who were in the camps were not called because that is what is done. There were some who returned wounded, with parts of their bodies frozen, but many of those recovered, because k'g'hrah are used to the cold.

CHAPTER 7
Far from the K'g'hrah Mountains

The caravan had been traveling for some days; they had left the cold keegrah mountains far behind. The keegrah had become silent again, and this time even the offer of a tale from the shashigai did not loosen his tongue.

Reticent and angry, the keegrah did nothing all day but stare into space, play with his flute, and fiddle with the bead on the red string around his neck. He grunted when they brought him food, but talked to no one.

Zev finally had to remind the keegrah of his promise to tell his story.

It is time to talk again?

We are far from the mountains. I don't want to go to Ethkell. I know that it will be easy to fly home from there. I would be more comfortable in my cave, where I was until you came over the edge of the cliff. You would have been warm. I would have given you furs.

I have tirothi and sarkoth furs. I've had them in the cave for many summers; they don't have many bugs, just the little white worms and the tiny black jumping bugs. They bite but if you roll in the snow they go to sleep. Sometimes there are spider mites but when I get those I stay in nok and roll in the snow. The spider mites are easiest to get rid of but they bite the hardest and the places where they bite itch for many days –

You are scratching again.

After Merinell I went to the mountains above Cnieren, and I stayed there until after Ethkell, and after that was when Al-Medi called for me. Then I went to Ak-Shamalim and then I saw her dance.

Oumid will tell you that Marai danced all night, just like the dancers. They are strong, those desert tribes. Hers was called Canni – she probably was related to the Dekani – they are the lowest of the Tuklos tribes. You are a shashigai but I do not know your position at Tuklos. You have the sharp teeth, so I know you are from there. There are the Vahtani, the historians and the tapestry masters, but you are not of them, or you would be fat and useless or else a military general. There are the Esgeni, but you are not of them – you are not pale and weak, and you are not draped with jewels. You are not Dekani, or you would not be a grehti.

But you only say that you are from the tribe of the shashigai. I did not hear of you when I was in Tuklos. I heard of caravans of entertainers, but they did not call them tribes. You are more than a storyteller if you can persuade the grehti.

You are allowed to have your secrets. I don't care. I only care for the day that I fly free from this caravan and never see your face again. You are not the sky. You travel on the ground, through trees, and that is hard for me – it is not easy to open k'g'hrah wings among the trees. I think you have done it to trap me here.

I will tell you more of the story, so that I may arrive at its end.

The night that Marai danced, many men asked who was her father, and they tried to find out because there were many offers to pay her bride price. This made the other girls angry because they had come with their ornaments and oils and perfumes to get the men to offer for them. Marai was a girl from an uncivilized desert tribe with a rag in her hair, and she had broken taboo, yet still the men wanted her.

For some days there were fights among the men. This provided more entertainment, and sometimes more meat. The men who did not fight made wagers about who would win. This was because the red girl Marai raised their fires. Wealth does not matter when men's fires are high. Finally a few days later a group of men went to the grehti Al-Medi, who was the head of all Ak-Shamalim at that time.

A grehti by the name of Shavadi said that Akhad Rai was Marai's brother. Poor fortunes for the men, because Akhad Rai is said to be a demon in nok shape. They say he began as a bandit and then became a merchant, but he still fights as a bandit. He is a fierce warrior and shrewd trader and besides he is wealthy and his family is large and well protected. It is possible that he mated with someone from one of the desert tribes. If he claimed her, there would be trouble. The men backed down, but I think it was a lie. The grehti Shavadi was around her all the time after that. I think he said that about Akhad Rai because he had chosen to mate with her and because there was no father or brother to protect her.

This part of the story you must hear first. The dancers, they dance from the time the fires burn high until the dawn. Marai danced almost until then. There were two people from her tribe there – the girl Marai and a boy who became a warrior. There were supposed to be three. That was what we found out – she was dancing, her eyes closed, and her steps were in perfect time with the drums and the singing. It is as I said, if I had fire, it would have risen. She danced close to me, and I knew she was reaching out to me. I could not do anything but watch. So beautiful were her movements in the steps of the dance, every man was as if frozen.

A voice like the wind called, "Marai!"

She stopped. My heart fell as if into my feet.

"Where is my sister?" she cried, and at that moment, I heard a demon, a sperith, in the same voice, cry out the same words, and both voices were full of anguish and pain.

She whirled and ran looking at everyone there. Again and again, she cried, "Where is Mirabel?" The grehti women tried to hold her but she cried out and knocked them down.

I looked around. No one else heard the voice. It was a demon crying, and her voice was like Marai's voice.

It was like an echo, that voice, and I stood up to help her, the girl Marai, not the sperith. A grehti waved at me to get her, so I stood in her way as she ran. I guess they didn't care if I got knocked down. She did run into me, but she didn't knock me down. She grabbed my arms, and the grip was like that of a man. She looked at me and cried, "Where is my sister?" And the same words echoed behind me. I turned around, and there was a sperith fleeing because they were throwing wood on the fire.

Some rsakk warriors chased it. They lost it in the darkness. One came back with his arm frozen, and he could not move it for many days. Everyone was surprised that he was not frozen dead by the sperith.

At Ak-Shamalim and even in the child house men are trained in what to do with women. I put my arms around her. She fell against me and cried, and I stroked her hair. The grehti Shavadi looked at me with an angry look, and after that he was always around her. Well, not always. That is what this story is about, yes? Not about Shavadi and Marai, but about Oumid and Marai.

The grehti could have told this story to you. You are a grehti. Why did they send you to me?

They will not tell you? Do they know I am telling you?

Of course I am laughing. The grehti, for all their wisdom, lack the sense of a k'g'hrah at times. They think that talking about the speritu calls them. I have talked to them and that does not call them. They only come when they are hungry. You are not a real grehti so I can tell you that the grehti are foolish sometimes. They have the power to fight the demons, but they would rather see rsakk and k'g'hrah die fighting them. They do not know the nature of the speritu. But they wanted to know, and that too is part of the story of Oumid and Marai.

They asked me to catch the sperith.

CHAPTER 8
What to Do with Women

Marai asked first.

I blame the dance for making me forget that I am k'g'hrah. I blame the red girl's beauty. When she looked into my eyes, I forgot many things. I forgot Kgh'jsh k'g'hrah. I forgot even the sky, and the wind's voice. I became Oumid. Oumid-rsakk, who would give anything to have the beautiful dancer Marai as his mate. But Oumid lives on what Kgh'jsh earns. I had nothing to give for a bride price. So I gave her something more valuable than jewels or bracelets.

I gave her my word. I promised I would help her find her sister.

I think it is the same thing that binds me to the sky, that thing that makes me hold to my promise. That is why I do not give my promise easily.

The next day, I regretted what I had done in the night. I did not mate with her, yet I was bound to her by my promise. It was possible that she would leave or the grehti would ask me to go somewhere else, but if not I would have to help her find a sperith.

I heard that she went to the women's compound and the mothers there punished her for disrupting the dance. I think they were jealous. The women in the compound all had oils and perfumes and skirts with embroidery and ornaments to make them pretty, but I think no man ever looked at them the way the men looked at Marai that night.

They punished her, but she did not repent, and that was how we met again.

You know that cliff at Ak-Shamalim where the k'g'hrah soldiers train? The one that has all the caves and holes in it? There's places there that are k'g'hrah only, you can only get there by flying. Well, you could get there by climbing, but all the rsakk know better than that. It's easy to fall and if you are not k'g'hrah, you will die.

Marai didn't know better.

They were giving her the worst things to do, which is normal since she wasn't going to be anyone's first wife. They had her grinding the meat and she had to go with the children to the nethik village for the water carts. That's a foul job to a rsakk because they don't like water.

To get the water you have to stand in the river so the jugs will fill, and the nethik make the new ones do it themselves. She didn't seem to mind that.

The mothers were beating her too, and she fought back so it took more than one of them to do it. She did not know that it was part of the training. It's hard for the girls from the tribes. They don't go to a child house so they aren't trained to be submissive. They're wild things. Marai was strange for a wild girl. She didn't seem as wild as the stories, and she learned some things really fast. Like how to speak the language of Tuklos, and how to sew and cook. After a moon or so she wasn't getting beatings as often and her woman skills put the other girls to shame. But they did not allow her to see the dancers again.

She ran away a lot, and she didn't care that they beat her when she came back, and no one could find her when she ran away.

I was still staying at Ak-Shamalim there because the speritu kept coming back. It was a bad thing. Ak-Shamalim had never had a plague of speritu before. Every night I was out flying. After morning prayer I would go up to my camp – that was one of those holes in the cliff – and sleep until evening prayer.

On one morning like that I dropped onto the ledge and shifted back to nok – it's so hot down in the badlands that most people don't stay in their shape unless they're rsakk. I had a sleeping cloth and not much else in my cave. The cave went back far enough that the sun wouldn't reach it, and it had room for supplies but I didn't need those. All I had there was my flute, and some rsakk clothes that they made me wear when I came to prayers.

I pulled the sleeping cloth around me and fell asleep – almost. There was a noise from the back of the cave where my clothes were. That made me angry – one of the rsakk, I thought, teasing me by putting a critter in my place to mess my clothes so I would have to wash them before evening prayer. I had chosen a cave that was a hard place to get to because they had done that before. I was thinking that they must have gotten a k'g'hrah to help them.

But when I went back there, it wasn't a critter. It was a woman sobbing. It was Marai.

"How did you get up here?" I asked, but she kept on crying.

I thought of my training, what you do when a woman is crying, and since it had worked before I put my arms around her.

I held onto her as long as I could. It seemed a very long time because my arms were getting stiff, and then she suddenly pushed me away and was staring at me. I got worried and felt around on my skin, but I didn't feel any mud or bugs. I was glad because I didn't want to give her scale mites.

"You're not wearing any clothing!" she said.

I got confused and looked outside. It was still daylight.

"It's not time for evening prayer," I said.

She looked at me kind of funny then, and said, "Oh."

But she wasn't crying anymore.

I remembered from my training that I was supposed to ask her what was wrong, or what she needed. I wasn't her husband and I wasn't rsakk so I wasn't supposed to slap or bite her when she cried.

"Is something wrong?" I asked.

"Could you put that on?" she asked and she was pointing at the sleeping cloth, so I wrapped myself in it and laid down and went to sleep again.

But I didn't get to sleep at all. She slapped me on the back of my head. I sat up because it stung. She had strong arms for a woman.

"Why did you do that?" I asked.

"Don't you like me?" she asked.

I looked at her, and even though the cave was dim I could still see her hair. The mothers had taught her how to use the oils and combs and although her hair was thinner than when I had first seen her, it was still very pretty.

"Yes," I said, "I like you very much."

"You were watching me during the dance."

"Everyone was watching you."

"But you didn't offer to buy me."

"I don't want a rsakk wife. I am a k'g'hrah."

That made her smile.

"I wouldn't mind someone to talk to. I hate it here!" she said. I didn't know what to say about that so I waited.

"But I like it here too," she said, "Something in the air – or the food. I don't know. Maybe it's the music. I feel like I'm at home."

"Does your tribe play music?" I asked.

"My tribe is very far from here, and very different."

I nodded. She continued to look at me, and then I realized she probably wanted me to say something else.

"Um." I said, but I knew that would not be enough, so I said, "I don't like it here either."

"You don't? But you're a mercenary. Why don't you quit and go home?"

"I can't."

"Why not?"

"I told them I would help them. I gave them my word. I am unable to take it back."

"Why not? Just give them their payment back."

"I cannot change my words. It is how I am."

That made her go quiet for a long while.

So I went to sleep again.

She slapped my head again.

This was a problem, because I didn't have anything in my training about being slapped in the head by a rsakk woman. I heard that tirothi women do it all the time, both in shape and in nok. It's worse when they're in shape – I guess to another tiroth it wouldn't be bad because of all that fur. But for tirothi women, the men slap them back and yell and then they yell and slap the men back and it goes on like that until they get tired of it. Nethik women can be slapped but they are not supposed to slap you. K'g'hrah women don't slap, but if a man makes them angry and then fails at his hunt, he will go hungry when he comes to the serving place.

I was thinking about this and wishing I could go talk to Al-Medi because he had given me some good advice about women in the past. However, he had not told me what to do if I was slapped by a rsakk woman.

That left me with the thought that she was rsakk and there was nothing in my training about a k'g'hrah being slapped by a rsakk. If I were rsakk I could bite her or knock her down, but I am not rsakk. I did guess that she didn't want me to go to sleep, so I sat up, but she grabbed my hand when I tried to unwrap my sleeping cloth.

"I don't want to mate," I said, and she made a gasping noise and tried to slap me again.

This time I caught her hand and did not let her do it.

"Please don't hit me again," I said to her, "I am not sure what you mean by it."

She made a sound that the mothers made a lot when I was in child house, so I guessed that she was frustrated. They made that sound a lot for me.

I remembered something from that first night, and I thought it would help her, so I said, "I will keep my word to you. I will help you find your sister."

She made a happy noise then, and I was glad because it seemed like until then I had been doing a lot of things wrong.

And then she hugged me and knocked me down (which was odd but I liked it) and we did something that was like mating except we didn't mate. She called it wrestling. It was – fun. I wanted to do it again, but I had to sleep. I was sure that she would get a beating from the mothers, because when I woke up for evening prayer, she was still there, and she had wrapped the sleeping cloth around both of us.

CHAPTER 9
The Promise of a Wife

The grehti's request was not a promise. The grehti
Shavadi was in charge of the shapefound celebration, but
he was not in charge of Ak-Shamalim. Did I say that
they train grehti there? Ah, you know that, you are one
of them. Well, at that time they had people training there
like they have at Eileah, which is the best and oldest
training place. At that time Ak-Shamalim was a good
place to go if you were a grehti. They have many more
kinds of demons at Eileah, and bad weather in the cold
months besides. The head of the grehti enclave was Al-
Medi, and he was in charge of the grehti for Tuklos and
ones for the desert tribes that were large enough to have
a priest assigned to them.

Shavadi-rsakk was in charge of training the men who were not going to be warriors or grehti. Garad-grehti, from the north, trained both at Tollach and Eileah – he was in charge of training the k'g'hrah and thank the Mother he was a k'g'hrah himself. He got me out of some trouble. The grehti who oversaw the training of the women was Mother Shiri.

Mother Shiri was the first wife of Al-Medi, and part of her work was to show the women how to be a good first or second or third wife. Because Al-Medi loved Mother Shiri, he paid no attention to who was chosen to be trained. The first wife was chosen already; an Esgeni had arranged it for his wife-to-be. Al-Medi chose the rest from ones Mother Shiri picked out, and she changed them all the time. It was said to be good training for the girls, but others said her training was harsh. The girls competed to get into the house of Al-Medi, though, because it made them more valuable to their husbands and fathers and brothers to have been there. It could raise a woman's bride price, and a woman who had no one asking for her could find her circumstances changed by going there.

Marai was the first one I ever saw chosen by Al-Medi. Usually Mother Shiri brought the girls before him, and they stood in his presence, showing all the charm that could be brought forth by girls of fourteen summers. Some of them had been trained well in the child houses; they could raise the fire of a man just by appearing before him. But Al-Medi paid no attention, and Mother Shiri told him who to choose.

I was there with some other k'g'hrah. Guards were needed because of the speritu; the girls had to be moved safely from their compound to the grehti compound and back. Only those girls chosen by Al-Medi (Mother Shiri, actually) would stay in his tents.

He looked at the girls and talked a little with his priests, and the girls waited quietly (for once) while he walked among them and looked at their arms and legs and breasts and teeth. And Mother Shiri walked with him and in front of some she said, "This one is well trained," and in front of others, she said, "This one would be good in the kitchens."

Al-Medi walked back and forth, and he chose two for the kitchens and one who was well trained, and then walked back to his cushions. Mother Shiri went to his side and reminded him, "You must choose one more for a third wife."

Al-Medi pointed at the one who was well trained and said, "That one is the third wife." The girl, her name was Yaida, got a sad look on her face and cried quietly.

Mother Shiri got a frown on her face and said, "Then you have to choose a second wife."

Al-Medi looked at her and said, "Where is Marai?"

Marai had been left at the women's compound, and Mother Shiri had given her the job of washing out the dung pits. Girls must not smell and their compound must not smell, so, unlike the men, the women had a pit, and Marai's job was to climb down into the pit and fill the dung buckets, then wash out the rest with water.

She'd finished that job, and she was in her quarters making marks in the sand when I went to get her. That was, of course, to keep the demons away. I told her what good luck she had that she would be second wife of the head of Ak-Shamalim.

"I don't want to be anyone's wife," she said, "I told my mother I would not marry anyone."

"Your mother?"

"Um," she said, and I realized that the desert tribes were indeed uncivilized as they had told us. It sounded like the mother was in charge!

"My brother will not accept any bride price for me," she amended. By then we were walking toward the grehti compound, which is at the opposite end of Ak-Shamalim. It was a nice, cold night. That was one of the things that made having to be at Ak-Shamalim better. Badlands nights can be as cold as some of the cold seasons in the mountains. There was a moon just rising – the pale, red moon Fyri.

It was just after evening prayer. She walked slow, that girl. It was because she didn't understand that any position in the house of Al-Medi is an honor. She would be trained as a second wife in the house of a high grehti. No one could hold her place of birth against her after that. Yet she dragged her feet through the sand and walked slow.

I refused my wife. They bought a girl for me even before my shapefinding, and I told them I wanted to be a grehti priest. They were amused. They left me alone. They knew I would not be a jewel merchant like the Esgeni, and at that time no one from the Vahtani had spoken for me. So that girl went back to her house.

Marai didn't understand. I tried to explain it as we walked, and she kept saying that she did not want to be the wife of any man. She was a strange one. It was wrong of her to refuse to be any man's wife. Still, that gave me a little hope, because by then I had begun to think about what it would be like if I were to have a wife.

It would mean mating, of course. That might not be so bad with someone like Marai. She was pretty even before they made her teeth sharp. She was smart and she didn't talk much. Especially important was that she could climb up to my cave with no help. There are some rsakk who can do it, but she did it in her nok shape. Since her color was red, it would have been easy to see her climbing in shape. So she covered her hair and climbed with nok hands and feet all the way up to my cave! That is a good thing.

When I went to the women's tents to call her to the grehti, Marai spoke to me in a tone much like the mothers used when I had done something really bad.

"You weren't there!" she said, and it sounded like the girls when you give them a present that isn't good enough. That is not a good thing even if you do not want a wife, because there are times when it is hard not to look for someone to mate with, and at those times you want the girls to like you.

"Where?" I asked, because I had not agreed to meet her anywhere, especially not with Shavadi watching.

"Your cave!" she said and her voice was like the not a good present voice.

Now I realized the problem. She had gone back and climbed up to that other cave, thinking it was still my cave. That night when I found her in my cave, I moved, immediately, after she left. It was a good cave, but she had made it smell of woman, and worse, of her. That would have been too distracting from my thoughts, and from playing my flute.

No, I am not religious. I understand the religion of the Mother, and why it is good for us. It is not good for me.

I prefer the smell of the sky. I think of the sky, my partner, who welcomes me when I have need of anything, or if I need to be alone. It is the sky who sings to me when I am in my cave.

When I have time and the sky is blue and the wind calls me, I go to be there. The greatest sadness I have is that in shape I cannot play my flute. So we live separately, the sky, the wind and I. I can be with one or the other but not both. At Ak-Shamalim it is hard to play the flute. Music is a thing left to the dancers. The k'g'hrah like the flute – the high pitched sounds are the way we call to each other when we are in shape. The tirothi like the flute too, though how it reminds them of their coarse screeching, I do not know.

I played when the sun came up; at that time it disturbed only a few. Then the wind and sky were close – the cliffs are very high – but it was not the same as flying.

How could I smell the sky with rsakk smell in my cave?

She did not understand. It did not matter. I did not have to talk about it anymore and Marai did not have to go to the tents of Al-Medi.

A demon came, a sperith, and it wanted Marai.

CHAPTER 10

Shapeless at Ak-Shamalim: The Demon

I heard it coming first, and when I heard it, I thought it was Marai crying again.

She was not crying. Her eyes were big and she pointed at the sperith – she could see it.

"Bel!" she cried, and the sperith cried "Marai!"

It wailed and dove straight for her.

I shifted quickly. The sperith touched her and she fell, but I grabbed Marai and flew up. The sperith followed.

Yes, I am the one who does that. That is one of the reasons they called me to Ak-Shamalim – to teach the others how to fly away from the demons. It is easier if you can hear them. The other technique is simple too. It requires strong wings and a strong stomach too. Since the demon was still following, that is what I did. I flew straight up.

During the day, that is enough to lose a demon – they do not like the sun – it burns them. But that night, with only the one moon, the demon was not afraid. It followed as fast as I flew.

So I flew into one of the k'g'hrah caves – the big barracks caves, where k'g'hrah sleep in shape. Seconds before I should have hit the wall, I shifted to nok and we tumbled to the ground. The k'g'hrah in the cave were amused until I called the alarm.

The sperith kept going – walls do not stop them – and it got lost in the walls. Most of the time that is enough.

They sent out patrols, rsakk and k'g'hrah with torches. This time, even with patrols and torches, it came back.

It was the same one – it called out in the voice of Marai, and it tried to touch her again. You, in your caravans with lights hanging all around and your big cook fires, you have not seen them the way I have seen them. They come from anywhere – out of the sky, up from the ground. They hide in the trees of a forest, and in rocks where you think you are safe.

There is one place, only one safe place for k'g'hrah, and that is the sky when it is blue. The demons, they do not like the fire of the sun. When I have the sun, I have no need of rsakk fire. The demons cannot reach me then.

The sky was dark that night. There were just the stars, and Fyri rising over the cliffs.

We had come down from the k'g'hrah cave and were again walking to the tents of Al-Medi, and Marai was quiet and walked very stiff and away from me. It came back again, the sperith, it came back crying, and this time up out of the ground. This time I was holding a torch, and it fled from the light and heat. But even after that I could hear it crying somewhere near.

Marai stopped and refused to go further. She stood for a moment looking at the place where the sperith had come out of the ground, and then she went there and touched the place. I pulled her away because it was dangerous, and she knocked me down. Since the sperith had not attacked her when she touched the ground, I let her stay there. I worried about Al-Medi. He was expecting her.

I reminded her of it.

"Marai, Al-Medi waits for you. He is important and not to be disobeyed."

In response, she sat on the ground, in the middle of Ak-Shamalim, in the middle of the night, and cried. There was alarm all around us and the fires being built up, so no one paid attention to us. She put her face in her hands and called "Bel" over and over again, which made me a little anxious because I knew she was calling the sperith. It could bring others with it.

There was a bad look on Marai's face, the kind those people got when their whole village was destroyed. That was Merinell, destroyed by speritu and fire. No one left, almost. Even the warriors, men from Ethkell, soldiers all cried to see the stiff bodies. Even their grehti did not escape; I found his body, frozen like the others. There is a protection spell, and his hands were in that position, but it did not help. All the worse, it was skydark. Shapefinding. Children who never would be men and women lay around what had been the fire. There was fear and confusion. Someone had run through the fire and scattered it. There was a girl there, a pretty one, in her shapefinding dress, and I asked her how she had escaped. She looked at me and ran away. I suppose she thought I was a sperith.

I found a mother there; I don't know how she escaped. I found her going from person to person, touching them, calling their names, covering their bodies with blankets. We took her to Ethkell, and she wept all though the long trip there, and she would not eat. She had seen the demons. She said their number could not be counted.

That woman, that mother. Her face carried a look that I have seen on the faces of those who were tortured. Marai had that look on her face, like that woman, as if she had lost all her tribe. She called to the demon, and it answered her. I could tell that she knew the demon.

I've heard of tribes that don't kill their shapeless. The grehti send some of their people with the caravans to reach them, because it's those demons that come to Ak-Shamalim. Marai must have been from one of those tribes.

Al-Medi sent Marai back to the women's quarters. No one wanted her there because they said she had called the demons. Some of the girls even said she had called the demons with her dance, and that the mothers should punish her again.

Mother Shiri was instructed to bring Marai to the tents of Al-Medi the next day, and that was how they found out she had mind powers. He looked into her mind to find out about the demon, and she looked into his. This she told me on a day when she had climbed up to the cave where I met her. I kept two caves after I realized she would keep trying to find me. I kept one for her to come, and one for myself and the sky.

I wish I had been there when she looked into Al-Medi's mind. I have always been told that no one can look into the mind of a grehti. Marai told me that she could feel him in her mind. She said it was like when the men get a woman who is not spoken for – there is no permission to ask, so they do as they like, and spoil her. It felt bad like that to her, so she looked into his mind and told him to stop. I wish I had been there. It would have been amusing. I was most surprised that he did not punish her for it. I have seen some that did bad things to the grehti, and the grehti made them shapebound, unable to shift, or worse, shapesick. I have seen them make a man as if his tongue was cut out, and there are some at Eileah that can shoot arrows of pain into the body of a man. But Al-Medi did not punish Marai in any of those ways.

Instead, he said she was to become a grehti.

After he talked to Marai, Al-Medi called me to his tent and looked into my mind. He was satisfied with what he found there. Maybe he liked the sky and the wind too. He told me that I was to find the demon that had attacked Marai, and kill it before the grehti caught it. They wanted to know more about it, and so they had been attempting to catch it with spells. But there was more. Al-Medi had found out something about the sperith that had attacked Marai. He told me not to tell her and I said that I would not.

It seems that he found out from looking into her mind that the sperith was her sister.

I didn't tell Al-Medi she already knew. He only asked that I not tell her that the demon was her sister, and so I did not.

There is another way end to a shapefinding, which you know, and that is to be found shapeless. People can become demons after they are found shapeless. Since they have no shape, they have no soul, and therefore the Mother does not protect them. This makes them vulnerable to demons who can come and take the place where the soul should be. So it is best to kill them so they cannot be made into demons and come back to kill people in your village.

Marai's sister had become a demon.

It was crying, and not like the demons who come hungry from the ground. It was crying like someone lost, alone.

CHAPTER 11
Sleeping Arrangements

They put Marai with the grehti women after that, because Al-Medi said she should become a grehti. I think Mother Shiri was unhappy about that, even though it meant that Marai would not be in the tents of Al-Medi. They went back to having a nethik clean the pits, and Marai's hair grew long and beautiful. She told me that Mother Shiri had been pulling it out as a punishment. I think she was pulling it out because Marai was beautiful. The grehti women liked her and they didn't pull out her hair or beat her. They knew they would not have to compete with her, because Al-Medi said that Marai would go back to her tribe and be a grehti there.

I was sad, I think, about that, because I had been thinking about what it would be like to have her come to my cave and live with me. Grehti women are always taken by grehti men. It would make it difficult, if not impossible, to have her come and clean my cave and cook for me and comb my hair and pick the spider mites out of my feathers.

It is hard to get spider mites out of my feathers. They make little sticky balls and live inside them and lay their eggs in the sticky stuff, and if something else (say, a scale mite) gets caught on the ball they pull it to the middle and eat it. They are only good if I have other bugs. If not, they come out of the balls and pull bits of my skin to feed on.

They make smaller sticky balls which are eggs, so if you get one spider mite then you will have many within a few days. If I ignore the pain, it is foolish, and if I don't clean them off, it is a sticky mess when I shift to nok. Some of the balls will fall off, but if they are biting when I shift, then they can get caught inside my skin.

Some k'g'hrah take sand baths. For me sand is hot and uncomfortable, and then the cave is full of sticky sand and spider mite eggs. Marai knew how to pull out the web balls with the mites still in them. She threw them over the ledge. I won't say where they landed, but a lot of the Tuklos girls learned how to get spider mites out of their hair that season.

Marai was already good at cooking when she came to Ak-Shamalim. The only thing she did not know was how to spice the meat. She complained about not having the food things that one finds where she lived with her tribe, so sometimes I got them for her, things like milk from the milk-taralk, which most rsakk would not drink because they say it makes their fires weak. I do not know about that because Marai's fires never seemed weak; she climbed very fast and she was very strong.

She made things that tasted very good with the things I brought her: grain cakes with berry fillings just like the nethik make up north. The rsakk at Ak-Shamalim do not eat grain cakes because they say they are nethik food. Still, some of them must have, because no one ever punished Marai for making them. In fact she complained that if she did not take a few from out of the coals, they would all be gone by the time she had let them cool.

I think also that someone must have told Al-Medi about the cakes because when she went to the grehti tents they brought her the things to cook them, only instead of berries they made her put spiced meat inside. While she was there she brought me cakes when she made them.

She said she was happy in the grehti tents. She said they treated her better. They watched her at first, because they said she was the one that called the demons. When she stayed there and no demons came, after a time they let her do more things and go out by herself. She was being trained by Al-Medi and by the grehti Shavadi. I was sure that Shavadi would mate with her; I saw his fire rise when she danced. It did not happen; she came out of his tent untouched, and later we laughed together when she told me about it.

Al-Medi was fair to his women; he let mother Shiri train them but he left them clean for their husbands. Or so he thought. Mother Shiri had agreements with most of the grehti and some of the girls; for the right price a girl could be trained by the one who paid. For some of the girls this was desirable, as they were going to houses where they would be in the kitchens, or where they would be the wives of men old enough to be their father's fathers. For others it was desirable to have their first experience be one where the man was gentle and did not injure them badly. The injury is part of the women's training, but mother Shiri did not follow the custom, which was to allow the husbands of the women to visit to train them.

The grehti Shavadi had an arrangement with mother Shiri, and so even though she was in the tents of the grehti it happened that one day that Marai she was told she would be receiving training from Shavadi-grehti.

She said that he told her that it was a privilege to be trained for the duties of a wife by a grehti, and an honor to bear a grehti child, and he was right. It is a high honor for a woman, and insurance that even if she does not have mind powers she will be accepted among the grehti as a lesser wife. Marai had mind powers. If she mated with the right male she could find herself at Eileah, where only the most talented are trained.

She would not do it. She told him that she did not
want to mate with him, or bear children, not his and
not those of any other man. That part I did not
understand. A woman is to cook and bear children, and
if she is rsakk, to draw the fire in the body of her mate.
Then the grehti Shavadi said that he would mate with
her anyway; this was his right as a rsakk. If she were
spoiled by the mating he would answer to her father or
her brother Akhad Rai, and pay her bride price.

Shavadi belongs to the house of the Tapestry
Master, so he was wealthy. Marai said that he showed her
his wealth and offered it for her father or her brother.
She told him it was worthless, and she said that when
she said that his face was as red as fire, but he did not
shift. He took her arms and forced her down. In this she
should have known her duties but she did not. It was
mother Shiri who should have been teaching her more
than punishing her.

Because she did not know her duty as a rsakk
woman, she fought back, and more than just for mating.
She did not shift because the mothers in the women's
quarters had not taught her that. Instead she did the
thing called wrestling with him, and slapped him, but
with her fist instead of her hand open. That was the part
we laughed about, because he fell down and did not get
up for a time after she slapped him. I laughed, but I was
glad that I had not tried to mate with her, because I
would have done so as Oumid who was raised as a rsakk,

and Oumid's head hurt a lot even when she slapped him with her hand open.

Shavadi could not complain; Al-Medi was not aware that such things went on. So Shavadi sent Marai back to the tents of the grehti women and said nothing to mother Shiri or to Al-Medi. Still he watched her, and when she was alone he would come and talk to her so that no other man was able to be alone with her.

Or so he thought.

She still ran away. Shavadi led morning and evening prayer for the men, because he was in charge of their training. When those duties were done he would go looking for Marai, and just like mother Shiri, sometimes he could not find her.

I had no reason to betray her. They asked me to look for her sister, not for Marai. And there were the spider mites to consider. They called me Oumid, but she said I reminded her of a man named Bonnus, who was her friend since childhood back in the Canni tribe. She would rub my head and tell me we could be friends like she was friends with Bonnus.

Sometimes I was sleep starved and her touch made me smile. It was one of those times that I agreed to be her friend. When I told Al-Medi that Marai said she wanted to be my friend, he said that it was a good thing to have a friend, and that it was good that I had said yes.

She did not ask, at first, whether I had found her sister. Perhaps she thought that I would tell her when I found the sperith, but I promised only to find it. It was better that way, I thought, because I did not know when I would find her sister, and meanwhile there would be no spider mites and many smiles.

I do not think she would have asked me to be her friend if she knew that I was going to kill her sister. But I had promised that to the grehti Al-Medi, so there was no choice about it.

During the days, when she could come to the cave, I spent time with her. It was fortunate that she did not come often. In those times it was hard to choose between Marai and the sky. I had many patrols because many of the Ak-Shamalim k'g'hrah were at Ethkell, building a camp to protect the city.

Fewer k'g'hrah at Ak-Shamalim meant that I was free to sleep on top of the cliff, and so I made a tent to keep off the sun but let in the sky, and there I played my flute and gazed at the sky. Without Marai there I remembered that I was Kgh'jsh-k'g'hrah and not Oumid.

During the nights I patrolled looking for speritu, and in particular the sister of Marai. We did find some speritu, and the rsakk who were patrolling with us burned them, and all that was left was ash. It's hard to tell one demon from another when all of them are reaching for you, moaning in hunger and pain. The rsakk say they are fearless, but they shrink away from the demons. I did not, because if I did I could not tell which one was the sister of Marai.

I hunted but not with all my energy; I was waiting for the next skydark. Skydark is the best time for demons to appear; there is no moon to frighten them, and some of the fires are not well kept. Skydark is the time when one is most likely to see demons.

However, in that time I did not have to wait for skydark to see the work of demons.

CHAPTER 12
Marai's Story

It was a summer skydark when Marai came to Ak-Shamalim, and the moons had both come and gone when she went to the tents of the grehti.

Things had calmed down. Mother Shiri still looked at Marai with anger, but mother Shiri was not the head of the grehti women. At this time, mother Shiri was busy with the hardest part of the training. Hard for the new women, not for her.

Rsakk heal fast. This is why they are formidable in battle. Some wounds heal quickly and others take days, but it is a thing they must learn or they cannot become good warriors. It is especially important for the women, because during mating they are torn and bitten and scratched, and they must heal from that if they are to provide proper service to their husbands. Without proper service, the fires die down and the warrior is useless.

It is a good time in the camp because finally after seeing the girls for at least a moon, we are able to mate with them. The ones who are bought are trained by the grehti priests, so they are not spoiled for their husbands, and the ones who are not are trained by the men. They set up tents for this purpose, and the women are brought there, and when it is finished the grehti women go in to touch the minds of the new women and teach them to heal the wounds of mating.

In this Marai was lucky; she had been trained already in healing by mother Shiri's beatings. Al-Medi tested her. Mother Shiri was unhappy during that time. Mother Shiri had the richest jewels and the nicest combs but if Al-Medi looked at a pretty girl then she counted how he did not love her. She cried aloud about it to the other grehti women. This is why she chose the ones to be trained in his tents, so that he would not be tempted by the pretty girls.

When Al-Medi came out of the healers' tents and said that Marai needed no other training, mother Shiri cried to the other women that Al-Medi would go in to Marai again. She sent three rsakk warriors with deep and intense fires, and said Marai should draw them.

Marai was from a desert tribe; she did not know our ways, and she was red besides. Most of the girls were yellow or green rsakk, and a few brown ones who would likely lose their bride price when it was found that they had Dekani blood. Red is how men want to be found, to us – I mean them – it is like fire without as well as within. Reds are big and fierce. You already know by her temper that Marai was like that.

The whole camp talked about it - the warriors who went in came out again, and they needed more healing than Marai.

I went in too, because Al-Medi wanted to know more about Marai's demon. He thought that since it came when she called it, that we could kill it and discover its nature. She would not talk to him about the demon, and her mind was guarded so that he could not enter or speak as he would to someone without mind powers. I wondered if that made Marai as powerful as the male grehti priests, but I did not ask because I knew such things are not said. Since she would not talk to him, Al-Medi said that I should mate with her if she wished it, and that if she did, and I did, that perhaps she would talk to me about her sister.

That was a long list, so instead I asked her, and she told me.

"We are twins," she said (as if the demon were still alive), "We spent all our time together in Dekan, and sometimes we went over to Tapolith to play in the market. Bonnus saved us a few times; he was big, like you, and the merchants were all afraid to lie about what we had done in front of him. Bel was more timid than me, though – she wore skirts and at home she preferred to sew instead of to spar. We shared a bed during the cold season – we shared everything. She was a favorite of some of the hunters when we got older, and she always shared the presents they brought her – choice bits of meat, herbs they found in the forest, or ground roots to make good stew. I shared my prizes from the Tizzy – I mean from contests. I won good drinks for us, and sometimes beads. Ma Canny – I mean, the mother, she said that either Mirabel or me would be the – the mother, and take care of all the children. I left it to Bel because I did not want to be a mother."

"What else would you be?" I wondered, and her face got the bad present look.

"I could be grehti!" she snapped.

"That's right," I said, "I forgot about that."

For the rest of that day she would not talk to me.

It took Marai three days to heal from her training with the warriors, because she only had cuts and bruises. The other girls, even with help from the mothers and the grehti, took more, sometimes many days. I went in to Marai on the second and the third days after she rejected mother Shiri's men.

On her third day of healing, I tried to talk to her, and instead she began to do the things woman should do when a man comes in to her. She said Al-Medi had taught them to her. On that day she asked if k'g'hrah men had fire to raise. I said no, and she said that we should try it anyway.

I found out that it is true, the rumors about rsakk women. When their fire burns, it is said, they can raise the fire even of a nethik. I did not know that I had fire until that day. With her, I felt something that must be close to it.

After that she was as if she had drunk many cups of ruka. She smiled and laughed and whispered things in my ear. She told me many things that I did not understand. It is odd that those other grehti never asked me to tell them. I would have, but since then I have learned that it is not good to tell a grehti everything.

I too felt like I had drunk many cups of ruka. At least that is what I think. I was dizzy. I could not feel the pain of the bites and bruises that mating with her left on my body. Neither of us shifted, but by the Mother! She was strong, and she bit me with teeth filed by grehti women. I wanted to mate with her again and again, but we did not have the strength, so instead we lay in each other's arms and she talked to me.

"Dekan isn't a tribe, it is a place," she told me. "That is where I learned to fight and that's where I had my shapefinding. We had it in the woods, where the moons couldn't be seen, and at a time that corresponded with skydark on Karn."

"There was me, and Bonnus, and Bel, and one other. Bonnus was big and he didn't understand, so he broke free and was in the woods in shape. The grehti came to test me and I looked into their minds – no one told me I shouldn't! And I saw what was to happen, and I warned him to run. I shouldn't have," she said sadly, and I knew then that she loved him.

It sounded like he had stayed in the desert with the Dekan tribe, so at that time I thought that I would not have to compete with him.

"They tested me and Mirabel together," she continued. "I found out that they didn't want to waste time on us, since not all of us have shapes."

That was a big surprise to me. I didn't know that they had whole tribes of shapeless. It makes sense now that we kill the bandits even if they have not stolen from us. I still do not understand why they did not kill her tribe if so many were shapeless.

"That idiot Bonnus came back, and in shape, and there was a lot of confusion. The grehti who was with me said, 'This one is rsakk!' and then grabbed my hand and dragged me through the gate."

That confused me too. Perhaps her finding was in a village after all, and they dragged her through the gates of the village.

She continued, "Al-Medi was there, and people from Eileah. Everyone crowded through the gate and I did not know why until I heard them shouting about demons."

When she said that I guessed that she did not know that demons often come to the shapefindings – that is why the fires are built so high.

"We landed in hot sand," she said, "and we walked for two days, and we were here, in Ak-Shamalim."

That was confusing too. It sounded as if they had not come in through the gates, and unless you are k'g'hrah, there is no other way into Ak-Shamalim. It is built among the highest cliffs in the badlands, and there is a bridge after the gate, and rsakk soldiers guarding both.

"But my sister," she said, "my sister was tested when I was tested, and I did not know that she was here until the dance. They told me she was dead. They told me she died during the test. She is my twin. We were so close, it was as if we could mind-speak. And after the shapefinding, I could not hear her."

She told me that her sister looks like her, except her hair is not red, and her sister was not so big and strong as Marai. From the description, I thought that her sister would have gone to the kitchens if she had not died and become a demon. Marai thought that her sister must be shapesick, and that there would be a cure.

She had not talked to the grehti about her sister because Al-Medi told her not to talk to anyone but him. So she could not know that the only way to cure the shapeless was to kill them. I did not tell her this; it would have spoiled her time of fire.

It did make me wonder. If her tribe had all those shapeless people, and they were not all killed like the people at Merinell, then it must be that not all of them had become demons. I thought about that until my head

125

hurt, and then I stopped. The grehti Al-Medi knew this tribe of hers and so probably knew all that she was telling me. So when he asked what I had learned, I told him about her sister. I did not tell the rest because I am very uncomfortable when my head hurts, and I had already been uncomfortable once that day.

For many days after that I was uncomfortable, and so was Marai, and likely all the grehti.

It was the next day that mother Shiri discovered the demon slain girl.

CHAPTER 13
The Demon Slain Girl

On that day, just before women's morning prayer,
mother Shiri went to the tents to make sure the girls
were up for their duties. They were to begin cooking for
the men who were not out hunting. I was in Marai's tent.
We were lucky it was not the first one, because we were
sleeping, still drunk with rsakk fire.

Mother Shiri's scream jolted us awake and we ran
out to find what was the matter.

Mother Shiri hissed and roared. When we found
her, she was in shape, and backing out of a tent. That is
what happens when you see a demon slain person,
unless you are me, and then you don't shift because you
know the danger is past.

The danger wasn't past.

I grabbed a torch and ran into the tent. A demon hovered over the girl's body, its hands stretching toward her face. I yelled and thrust the torch at it. It fled through the top of the tent, into the morning light. Its death cry raised the alarm.

The girl's name was Chaipa. She was from the tirothi jungles, but had been found rsakk, a green, at her shapefinding. Among the tirothi, the whole village is the family, and all of the tirothi in a region are considered to belong to the same tribe. It is possible that some rsakk who was shapesick or in trouble with his tribe fled there and sired her. In any case, she was beautiful, and her family was wealthy.

Chaipa had been bought by an Esgeni man, and she was to be his second wife, but Chaipa made sure everyone knew that he really wanted her for his first wife. He had sent the appropriate bribes to mother Shiri and to Al-Medi, and so she was chosen by mother Shiri to be trained in Al-Medi's tents as a first wife.

Mother Shiri did not like the girl, but the bribes were good ones, so she taught the girl all the knowledge of pleasing a man and of administering the household. Chaipa was allowed to order the other wives in their duties, and she was supposed to go in to Al-Medi for practice, but Al-Medi was not interested so he only mated her once, though because she was pretty he gave her many presents. Mother Shiri sent her to the healing tents since once was not sufficient training, but it was poor service to Chaipa's husband that she sent Tariq in to train her.

Tariq was cruel, and hurt her so that she took many days to heal.

Tariq was from the house of the Tapestry Master, like me. He was not chosen for leadership or for strategic battle. But he did seem to know what would do the most harm, and it did not matter to him if he harmed friend or foe. For that reason he did not have many friends, and for that reason he was kept at Ak-Shamalim – not just to keep him away from the military, but because there were some whose minds were closed to the grehti but not closed to the things Tariq could do to them. Tariq had been my littermate, but when I returned to Ak-Shamalim he did not acknowledge me so I did not talk to him.

None of the girls wanted to mate with him, so he was forced to go with the men who spoiled the kitchen wives. Because of this, he made an agreement with mother Shiri, that when she could, she would send him in to one of the pretty ones.

Mother Shiri sent Tariq in to Chaipa, but only the Mother knows why, because if she had not been demon slain, she surely would have told her husband about Tariq, and then mother Shiri would have been forced to return the bribes.

But now Chaipa was dead and frozen, and because I am not afraid to do such things, Al-Medi sent me to touch her and say if she was indeed dead. I found no sign of life. Mother Shiri stood by watching to ensure that no one touched Chaipa's jewels or clothing. If the tirothi rejected them, they would become the property of the grehti. They would, because who would want the clothing of a girl who called a demon to her tent?

Mother Shiri had nothing to worry about. The only missing jewel was her favorite, one she had worn about her neck – a pendant with a white jewel in it. The leather cord was there, but the pendant was not. That meant that someone could have taken it before mother Shiri discovered Chaipa. But Ak-Shamalim was closed, so they would find the thief soon enough.

The girl had been frozen stiff and hard. There was no warmth in her. Once the badlands sun rose higher in the sky, she would be laid out to warm so that her body could be arranged in the funeral position before she fed the fires for the last time on Karn. Her spirit would return to the Mother. Perhaps next time she would not be so foolish as to do something to call a demon to her.

There were no other signs of demon work in the compound, and when the k'g'hrah and the rsakk and the grehti had all reported, it was found that in all of Ak-Shamalim, only Chaipa had been attacked. Suspicion fell on Marai, because she had been able to call one demon, and this was one demon's work. Al-Medi told them that Marai had been with me.

Mother Shiri warned me that if I smelt of Marai, the demons could find me in spite of my talents. I did not believe this, but I did go up to the cliffs and rub sand on

130

me where the smell was the strongest. Then I went down for morning prayer.

The chanting at morning prayers was not often enthusiastic, but on that morning it was even less so. The men's chant was very quiet and the women's chant could not be heard at all. The girls were subdued and frightened when they served the meat. I saw Tariq, and he looked afraid. He always said that he was not afraid of anything or anyone. He kept count of the demons he killed. He always refused to go on patrols with me because he said it was weak to enter a battle with warning where the enemy was coming. He always refused to go with me, but there were many that refused to go with him, because sometimes the ones that went with him did not come back. Tariq was fond of fire, and though it was the warrior's code not to use fire against fire, some said that when the demons were scarce, Tariq would hunt other prey.

On that morning Tariq looked afraid. I thought that he must have been to Chaipa's tent before the demon attacked her. Perhaps he thought about his own fate and what it might have been had he stayed with her. I knew from being drunk with Marai's fire why the men's morning prayer started so much later than women's prayer. I had barely been able to stagger out of Marai's tent when the alarm sounded. Tariq was a man of great fire. Everyone said that he would grow the second claw and become a great warrior. If he had been with Chaipa when the demon attacked, he might have been able to save her.

There was another surprise; he changed his seat to sit next to me on the rugs.

"They have ordered double patrols," he said.

"Mmm," I said between slices of meat, "that means I will be awake all of the night instead of just half."

"Garad-k'g'hrah has not chosen the patrols."

I nodded. "He will tell us tonight."

"He does allow those who work well together to choose their own partners."

"That is good of him," I replied.

Then Tariq got the bad gift look on his face. He looked around and then whispered to me.

"We should go together, we should patrol together."

I looked at him, and saw that he was not joking. I hoped that I had not forgotten what his face looks like when he is about to deceive me.

"You don't like me," I said.

To my surprise, he slapped his own head. I was glad that he did not slap mine. Tariq reached under his tunic and drew out a pouch. There were several jewels in it, but he closed it up very quickly so I did not see what they were. They were very pretty. Very shiny. He held the one he had chosen out to me.

"I will give you this."

I looked at the jewel in his hand. It was like the one that Chaipa had been wearing.

"Where is the finding?" I asked, because I thought it was like the one that had been part of the pendant.

"Finding?" he said. "There is no finding. I bought the jewel like this."

I thought the jewel looked too much like the one Chaipa had worn, and for that reason I told Tariq I would not take it. I did not want to call a demon to me. Tariq grumbled and returned the white stone to the pouch.

He pulled out another, and this one had a hole in it. It was not as shiny as the first one, but it was green and red and the red parts were like the color of Marai's hair. I had not heard of such a stone lost or stolen in Ak-Shamalim, so I said to him, "For that stone, I will go with you for one night." This was something Al-Medi had taught me, how to bargain for things.

He agreed and I took the stone and put it in my pouch, which until that moment had held a little stone whistle that I used to call to the sky. The whistle could hang on a string around my neck when I flew. I could make the red and green stone into such a whistle.

After that he went to sit with some other men and I finished my breakfast. I stayed longer to watch Marai serve.

Al-Medi called for me before the meal was done.

"Was it her demon?"

That was how he talked about Marai's sister. I did not think it had been, because neither Marai nor I had seen any demons that night. I had heard nothing, but Marai's tent was some distance from Chaipa's. Al-Medi also asked if I had seen anything suspicious and I said no, and he asked again, except the second time he said I should tell him if I knew whether anyone had gone into Chaipa's tent, or if I had seen her missing jewel. He also said I should tell him if anyone had said anything unusual to me. I am not sure why he asked those things, but they had easy answers.

I told him that I would be going on patrol with Tariq in exchange for a shiny stone, and I showed it to him, and he said that it was good that I had agreed to only one night. When I told him about Tariq going in to Chaipa's tent and about the white stone that looked like hers, he said that I should not tell anyone that I had told him. He also said that my usual patrol would not change; for the second part of the night I would fly with Tariq and patrol the sky above Ak-Shamalim. For the first part of the night, instead of evening prayers, I should stay with Marai to see if her demon sister came to her when the sun went down.

Marai was still in the healing tents and I had planned to go there anyway. Now I would not have to find something to trade with mother Shiri.

But I did not trade with mother Shiri that night. Other things happened.

If you look at the tapestries that describe what happened that night, they will speak of horror. People died.

CHAPTER 14
The Work of Demons

For the first part of the evening, I stayed in the tent of Marai, and for part of that time, mother Shiri was there because she did not want Marai to like me. But soon she was called to her own duties for evening prayer, and so I sat in the tent of Marai and I watched her.

"Are you expecting me to do something?" she asked.

Since I don't know how to watch for demons (I only hear them) I was watching her. She was pleasant to look at.

"I am not expecting you to do something, but Al-Medi expects you to call your sister, and then perhaps your sister will call the other demons, and we will know why they are coming here."

"Do you mean to ask them?"

"No. But Al-Medi will know what to do."

"Anyway," she said in the voice that means the gift was bad but she is pretending not to care, "my sister is not a demon. She's just shapesick."

Her hands clenched into fists, and even though I was not sitting near her I decided not to challenge her. She was fast and her hands hit hard even before she was trained in self defense. Women are never trained as warriors. If they were, Marai would have made a fine one. But on this night I did not want my head to hurt while I was on patrol, so I said nothing.

"You will still help me look for her?"

I nodded.

There was no reason I should not.

I didn't have a chance to look, though, because it was then, during second patrol, that the speritu came. It was an odd and sad thing. Usually the demons attack the men first – no one knows why. Then they attack any women in the area. I suppose that is why the attack the men first – the women are not kept near the battles.

It was mother Shiri who raised the alarm. She roared out that the demons were attacking and the signal torches were lit to show us where to land to fight them. I heard nothing this time, because they came out of the ground. But I saw mother Shiri running and she held in her hands a box. The girls ran behind her – those probably were her chosen ones. It was likely that the demons had attacked when she was teaching them some secret craft away from the other girls. When the demons came, mother Shiri's girls got away very fast. But the other girls and mothers got trapped in the women's tents.

It was the opposite of what we expected. In the past the demons looked for the men, or the grehti, or both. The patrols always concentrated on that side of the compound. But this time the demons swarmed over the women's tents and by the time we came from across the compound, several girls were dead and four others frozen with their faces twisted so that they did not look human. Most of the ones who had survived had shifted into shape, and burned the speritu (and the tents) around them. Some of the girls who were there and did not shift lived but were burned by rsakk fire. The women's fire training comes last, and only after they have passed all the other trainings, so most of the ones who shifted just blew fire everywhere and burned both demons and friends alike.

The mothers who were there shifted; that is why it was not a worse disaster. They saved many of the girls. Tariq screamed when I dropped him into the middle of the battle; he vanished in the flames, but later I saw him in the healing tents boasting about how many demons he had killed. I thought that was odd because after I dropped him I saw him running for the cliffs with some of the girls. I knew his shape because I had flown battles with him before, otherwise I would have thought he was

just some warrior escorting them to safety. I asked because I was curious, and he gave me a shiny stone for nothing at all and told me that he had gone back to the battle after escorting the women. This didn't seem likely because the battle was over very quickly, but as I said before, thinking about complicated things makes my head ache, so I stopped thinking about it.

A call went out to Tuklos and to the nethik village for healers; some of the girls who were burned had not had healing training. They called for the Tuklos healers because of the four frozen ones. No one at Ak-Shamalim had seen it before. The worst we had seen was a frozen arm or leg. These girls were completely frozen, yet mother Shiri said they were alive. She set Marai to watch them, and she sent for Tuklos healers because she did not want to touch the girls.

The nethik healers arrived quickly, but by the time they arrived Marai had kenned what to do for the frozen girls. She had them wrapped in furs, and already their limbs were loose enough that they could be laid in the funeral position. The mothers argued that this should be done because the girls were going to die.

But Marai said they would not, and she had pots of coals set inside the tents so that each one was as warm as if the sun was high. When they saw it, the girls who had not been injured asked to help, because the tents glowed red with coals. No demon would go near that.

By the time the sun rose, the healers from Tuklos had arrived. The speritu left us alone, but it was a long time before Al-Medi would allow us to stop patrolling. I knew he would call me, so after morning prayers I went to stand by the tent opening and that is how I heard him talking to mother Shiri.

"I've lost my taste for it," he said to her, and she made those noises you make to your pet to comfort it. "They will be sending word to Eileah for them to find another to lead here."

Mother Shiri agreed. That surprised me because I thought she wanted to stay at Ak-Shamalim.

"It is too dangerous," she said. "There will be another place where your skills are needed."

"It does seem like it would need a military mind. I have not been able to find out why the demons are attacking. The husbands whose wives died will call for my expulsion, or worse."

"We could leave before they reach a decision…"

"And risk the reckoners pursuing us to the end of our lives? Not only that, but the elders at Eileah will not allow us to leave before their judgment. No," he said, and his voice sounded sad, "we will wait for their decision."

"We?" she said, and she sounded frightened.

"You will share the judgment as will everyone in our house," he told her, and then there was a long silence.

"You have many friends in Tuklos." Now her voice sounded like she wanted to please him.

"Do I? All this time I thought it was *you* who had friends in Tuklos." Then I knew that Al-Medi was smart as well as kind.

"Use your influence! You are the head of Ak-Shamalim! You are high grehti!" Her voice sounded like the voice of Marai when she was angry.

"We will wait for their judgment," Al-Medi said.

Then there was a rustle of cloth that told me to stand away from the entrance. I moved in time to avoid mother Shiri as she stormed out of the tent. I waited for a little while, and then a servant came out of the tent. He looked surprised to see me.

"Al-Medi sent me to find you," he said, so I went in.

Al-Medi smiled at me but he looked sad. He said, "I guess we are in some trouble. Did you find the demon?"

"That demon was not there," I said, "and those others, they were crying that they had lost something."

"You understand them?" he asked, and I nodded.

"Sometimes I can hear them clearly. They are a lot like the sky. Sometimes I hear voices and sometimes there is just the movement of air."

"What are they saying now?"

"I don't know. I can't hear them," I told him.

"They are not here anymore?"

"I don't know. They are not near. That is all I can tell."

"Oumid," he said, and his voice was sad, "you can have some time off if you like. Go to the cliffs and play your flute."

"You do not need me?"

141

"I have looked into your mind, Oumid," he said, "and I know that you cannot hear the demons. As far as I can tell, you can sense their presence, but you cannot hear them. They are not crying to you, unless you mean the horrible noises they make when they are attacking."

I looked down at my feet, because at that moment it was hard to look at Al-Medi's face.

He was quiet for a while, so I knew he was thinking of how to explain it to me. I waited and finally he spoke.

"Oumid, it is certain that I will not be the leader of Ak-Shamalim after the people at Tuklos talk to the people at Eileah. They will not understand your talent, so you must hide it from them."

"Hide it from the grehti?"

"Yes, and any elders you talk to."

"I should hide it from you?"

Al-Medi sighed.

"Yes, from me too. We will not talk of it again. Say only that you seem to know when the demons are coming."

I nodded.

"Oumid, you are like a son to me. Did you know that?"

Even though I called him my father (which I only did because he was my teacher) I was surprised by that, so I looked at him.

"I have known you since your shapefinding. Back then I was worried about you; that is why I sent you to Tollach. I thought you would find friends among the keegrah." He laughed. "Even before you were

142

shapefound, we should have known it by your behavior."

He put his hand on my shoulder.

"Oumid, you are a keegrah among keegrah! You are the most keegrah-like man I have met in all my life. I like you for that. It makes you predictable, and dependable."

I had never heard words like that said about me. I looked down again.

"The Tuklos healers have sent for the Tuklos elders. We lost many of the women that belong to Tuklos men, and they will hold me responsible. The grehti will try to save me, but the Tuklos men will want some compensation for the promises I made to them as the leader of this place."

"They will kill you?"

"I hope not, but I think so. Go up to the cliffs and wait for them to call you. That way you will not have to talk to every curious person who arrives from Tuklos or Eileah. Talk only to the ones who are questioning the soldiers. Cooperate with them but do not tell them of your talent. They will ask you a lot of questions. Just remember what I said."

"I will," I said, and then I had to leave because a messenger from Tuklos had arrived.

.

CHAPTER 15
A Bad Time

I did as I was told. I went up to the cliffs. It was good
that I went up there, because there was a lot of
confusion at Ak-Shamalim that day. I heard that they
questioned all the warriors, k'g'hrah and rsakk alike, and
Tariq was questioned twice because he had gone in to
the first girl killed by the demons. New k'g'hrah soldiers
went back and forth between Tuklos and Ak-Shamalim,
bringing elders and husbands and brothers and fathers.
They came even though Al-Medi had declared Ak-
Shamalim closed. Then the Tapestry Master himself
came, and ordered everyone who was from Tuklos to go
back to Tuklos. He ordered the gates closed, and he set a
guard on the gates of Ak-Shamalim to kill any who tried

to leave or enter. The k'g'hrah who were already at Ak-Shamalim were called down to the compound and not allowed to fly. They grumbled because they had done nothing to deserve it.

All that time I was up on the cliffs, on a ledge near the top. I did not go to the top because the sun was too hot there. Instead I found a ledge where I could see a bit of the sky but not Ak-Shamalim.

It was a beautiful day, and the sky was very blue, but I was tired and could not have shifted unless my life was in danger. It was not, so I rested instead.

I rested and I played my flute. It was as if the sky knew of the sadness. The sky came and sang to me and it sounded like k'g'hrah mountains cool and high, and like cold water and taralk running across the meadows where they could be hunted. I played with my eyes closed, and I felt rather than heard it: the cool touch on my skin, and air passing over me like the wind in the k'g'hrah mountains. It called me to play more music. I played in the notes of the k'g'hrah, but I played the melody of the fire dance because that is what I knew best. On that day, for the first time, I could feel the sky dance around me as I played, and I was comforted.

Marai came to the ledge too; she was removed from her job of caring for the frozen ones, because they found out that she was from the desert tribes. They have a lot of anger in Tuklos at the desert tribes because they think most of the demons come from there, from those who do not follow the guidance of the Mother. Because they do not follow the Mother, they do not hold shapefindings, and they allow the shapeless to go about in the world. Many demons are said to come from this practice and the Tuklos men did not want their women attended by demon kin.

So Marai climbed up the cliff and onto my ledge and asked if there was anything she could do for me.

I wasn't injured, just tired, so I told her no. In spite of the fact that she knew I had been on patrol and in the battle, she hit my head. Her hand was open so I knew that she was not very angry with me. I thought she might be less angry if I said she could stay on the ledge with me, so I said that she could. She smiled after that.

It was all day before I felt all right to go down to Ak-Shamalim. I was glad of Marai's company on the ledge, because even though I was not in shape she pulled her fingers through my hair as if she were looking for spider mites, and that felt good. When I fell asleep she wrapped my sleeping cloth around me and shook the sand off my prayer clothes, so when I woke to the sound of the prayer bells, I could be on time for prayers, and clean.

When I went down for prayers, they saw me and asked why I had not come for questioning.

"No one called for me," I said, and because of Garad, the captain, I did not get into trouble. He explained things about me to them and they were satisfied and did not punish me. Still, they said that I should stay in the compound like the other k'g'hrah and that I could not fly.

That was the beginning of a bad time at Ak-Shamalim. They closed the gates to everyone, even the nethik, so many of the elders and the grehti had to be without their servants. New k'g'hrah had come to take the place of the ones that had been in the battle that night; no one explained why, and later Garad was sent away too. That was a mistake; the one who came was a k'g'hrah from Tuklos and he did not know how to order the patrols to watch for the demons. After a few demons were seen and the k'g'hrah were not properly mobilized, Garad came back by himself; he had to train the new k'g'hrah. I do not know what happened to the other k'g'hrah. I think they must have gone to Ethkell, because they were building a camp there. Garad told me that they were suspicious of some of the k'g'hrah and when I asked what they thought those men might do wrong he rolled his eyes and did not answer me. They did not send me away and later I found out that Garad had said that I should stay.

The elders of Tuklos went away and talked to each other, and the elders of Eileah talked to each other, and then people came from many other places and talked to the elders of Ak-Shamalim.

The girls who were frozen lived, but they were not right after that, so they were considered part of the lost. Altogether there were nine lost. The elders used words like devastating and tragedy, but there were still a lot of girls there. Even some of the pretty ones had survived. There was some fear that they would become demons, so there was some discussion of killing them. Instead, because they were all spoken for, all but one went to the houses that had paid their bride prices. The last girl was refused by her house, and her bride price returned. Her father did not want her either, so she stayed at Ak-Shamalim. One day she ran away. Since the gate was closed she jumped from a cliff and escaped to the Mother.

A surprise happened. Chaipa was healed by the Mother. She had been put in the sun to warm, and her body had not warmed past being able to be put in the burial position, so they put her in one of the healing tents and sealed it and forbad anyone to go in there. When the other girls were attacked, everyone forgot about her. A few days after the unwanted girl jumped from the cliff, there was a tearing sound from the tent where Chaipa was laid. The tent was torn in many places and Chaipa came out through the opening she had made. She was still very sick; when the sun touched her she screamed and fell down and was unconscious again, but this time they put her in one of the open healing tents and the healers came and said that she just needed rest and a little bit of light at a time.

Mother Shiri also surprised us. She too ran away from Ak-Shamalim. She ran away the night after Chaipa woke up. It was also just before the people from Eileah and the people from Tuklos were to come and talk to the elders of Ak-Shamalim about what to do about all the girls that had been lost. The gates were open by then,

149

but only during the day and only to certain people. Word had gone out to Tuklos and the tribes about what happened, and the caravans went to Tuklos instead of to Ak-Shamalim; we had to send servants there to trade with them. She must have gone out with the servants, because she was there for evening prayer, and it is after prayers that the servants leave and the gates are closed for the night. Mother Shiri did not go with the mothers to wake the girls the next morning, and she did not appear in her place to lead the prayers. Marai told me that. Marai said she guessed mother Shiri ran away because she heard that the elders would kill Al-Medi and his family.

After mother Shiri was gone they searched her tent, and even Al-Medi was surprised to see the wealth she had accumulated. The elders declared that she must have taken some of it with her and so they said she was a thief and if found she would be punished. Even so, they did not call the reckoners.

There was enough left to satisfy the bride price of all the girls of Ak-Shamalim and probably Tuklos as well: many shiny and many large jewels, more than I had ever seen, even in the markets at Tuklos. There were findings made of soft and hard metal, and bars of the shiny yellow metal the tirothi use to make jewelry. Al-Medi was not suspected in this because mother Shiri had hidden these things in her tents in the women's compound where the men cannot go. They had not found them by going into Al-Medi's mind. They only found them because mother Shiri was gone. There were ten chests, and two of them were empty; that is why they thought she had taken some of her treasure with her. Tariq had taken from the other chests; they caught him going back for more.

They would have killed him, but he had been useful to the grehti, so they made an example of him; they only punished him by making him shapebound for a time. They had the grehti from Tuklos do it because Al-Medi was under suspicion and not allowed out of his tent. The Tuklos grehti made Tariq stand in front of all of us and said that it was a warning that we were not to take anything that was not given or not already in our possession. Then he looked into Tariq's mind and broke the part that knows how to shift.

Tariq screamed and fell down, and had to be carried to the healing tents. When he woke up they made him do the things a servant did, and because he could not shift he could not run away and he could not fight. The grehti treated Tariq better than he had treated the servants, but Tariq had to stay with the servants, and they treated him well, though some spoke of doing to him what he had done to them.

The elders talked to each other a long time before making their decision, but everyone else said that at least Al-Medi would be shapebound, and probably killed. I was worried about this because Al-Medi had given me a lot of good advice; none of the other elders gave me such good advice as Al-Medi. The people said that the grehti Shavadi would become the head of Ak-Shamalim. I thought that if he did I would go somewhere else and just be k'g'hrah instead of staying at Ak-Shamalim, because I did not like him the way I liked Al-Medi.

I thought that I should take Marai back to her tribe and live in the badlands.

In those days the caves and ledges were good places to be. The new k'g'hrah all slept in the barracks cave, and unless they were training or on patrol they did not fly. They trained in nok shape too, learning to shoot arrows that set fire to bundles of wood, and to fly with torches that burned bright even during the day.

Some of the grehti who came taught us these things. They had learned them from the speritu attack at Merinell. Before the speritu came in great numbers to Ak-Shamalim, there had been many isolated attacks by demons, and the woman who lived from Merinell told the elders at Ethkell that such attacks had happened before Merinell was destroyed. So they thought that the demons would come back and destroy either Ak-Shamalim or Tuklos, or both.

There were torches and practice day and night and smoke from the fires often made the sky a color that was not blue. It made me unhappy. They sent k'g'hrah with me to learn how to listen for the speritu, but I could not tell them how I listened. Garad said that I should patrol every day and listen for the speritu, but I never heard anything more than the song of my sky.

I went up to the cliffs often. I felt bad because Marai could not come. They decided that she should be watched, even in the tents of the grehti, so someone always was with her. I played my flute for the sky instead, but although I felt its touch, it did not feel as it had before. The sky cried and sang to me of loss. There were thoughts and feelings as if the sky could mindspeak. The sky was sad and hungry. I could not comfort the sky as I had comforted Marai. So I played my flute and the sky danced and sang and cried. And we both waited for something to change.

CHAPTER 16
Mother Shiri Escapes: What No One Saw

Mother Shiri shifted back to nok. The caravan was nearby; once she got there she would be able to hide among the women in their cook wagons and child tents. She'd done business with the caravan owner in the past: the keegrah that had picked her up during the chaos of the elders' visit to Ak-Shamalim was from that caravan, sent by the owner at Shiri's request. The keegrah was a silent fellow who asked no questions and did as he was told.

Mother Shiri didn't care how the caravan owner had gotten the keegrah to violate the orders of the grehti to retrieve her, and she didn't care how much it would cost. She had taken in her pack a small fortune in gems — enough to pay for many such trips. The caravan leader had conducted her on more than a few trips between Ak-Shamalim and other places in the past. But there would be no more such trips for her, clandestine or in the open. She would never return to Ak-Shamalim. Let those fools think she had abandoned her fortune in panic. She had brought enough gems to live on for the rest of her life.

And she had the box and the gem.

The foolish mixed-breed girl Chaipa had given them to her, partly as a bribe – she wanted to be spared the worst of the healing training. Most of those who had not been raised among the rsakk wanted to avoid the training, and the easiest way to do it was to bribe the mother in charge. Most of them never realized that it was supposed to be their husbands who did the training, and it was their husbands who should arrange for substitutes. Mother Shiri took money from both the husbands who could not visit and from their fearful brides-to-be.

The other shapes had far less in the way of healing abilities, but no exceptions were to be made to the training – for mother Shiri that made for even better bribes. But the girl Chaipa had given mother Shiri something far more valuable than any bribe she had received. Yet all she asked was for assurance that the gem would be destroyed. It was a tirothi heirloom - a gem that could call demons.

Mother Shiri had been careful to only open the box during daylight, when the demons could not come. Indeed, the gem was ugly – it roiled with dark colors and glowed the same blue as the speritu. No trader would touch it. No matter. She was not going to sell it to a trader.

Testing the gem on the tirothi girl had been smart. The girl had been too ill from her time with Tariq to notice that mother Shiri had changed the stones. The demon had come immediately. Unfortunately, it had not been possible to kill the demon – that part of the reward would go unclaimed. And she had been unable to return Chaipa's gem to its original finding. But the demon jewel was safe in the box, secure until she could present it to Cailtoh, her contact at Eileah. By then, Al-Medi would be dead, leaving her free to pursue an alliance with Cailtoh who had power beyond that of Al-Medi. With his power and her wealth she would have guarantee of a comfortable life. She would live at Eileah, the most elite of the grehti enclaves. No more training spoiled whining girls who only wanted to learn enough to become first wife – as if drawing a man's fire was all they needed to know. No more kitchen training, no more uncouth desert girls in rags, sent by tribes who could barely afford the Ak-Shamalim price, who scraped together everything they could in hopes of a chance at nobility.

Ha!

She would build a household of real wives who were skilled at running the household and at kitchen work. She would never set foot in a kitchen again.

She stumbled.

The desert wind had grown cold. It whipped at her robe and lashed sand and stones at her feet. She stopped and set the pack down (last time carrying!). There was a warm cloak in there, and she put it on. Mother Shiri shouldered the pack and shivered as the wind grew even colder. They would have hot ruka at the caravan. The wind was like ice on her feet.

Ice?

She gasped. Icy fingers reached through her warm cloak. A cold hand grasped her thigh. A frigid arm wrapped itself around her waist. Icy cold gripped her arms but she shook free. Running, she ripped the pack from her shoulders and shook out the contents.

Her own gems, in pouches and sorted according to size and color, tumbled out. But an uncovered, ugly, glowing gem also tumbled out, confirming her fears. She hesitated – the others could be lost, but this one –

An eerie shriek, and then a wail, split the night as the box fell out next. She grabbed for it and turned to retrieve the gem, but too late. Blue figures roiled and swirled in the air and around the gem. Now they swarmed over her, grasping, freezing, sucking life from her. Her scream was cut off by a hand reaching down her throat. The broken box tumbled to the sand. Mother Shiri fell beside it, half shifted to rsakk, her face contorted by fear and pain.

The jewel rolled, pushed by a myriad of glowing blue hands competing to grab it.

It tumbled to a stop a short distance away. It pulsed — not with fire, but with inky, oily colors lit by a blue glow from deep within the stone.

Distorted blue figures rose from the ground around it. The ones sliding pale fingers over and into the body of mother Shiri turned, one after another, toward the stone. They flew to where the other figures already were fighting to grasp the stone. First this one, and then that one tried to touch it. Their fingers went through the stone, but tendrils of blue energy twined around their fingers and into their bodies. They pulled and tore at each other to get closer to the pulsing blue energy. Shrieks of triumph were indistinguishable from wails of pain and defeat. Perhaps even Oumid would have been frightened by it. But the noise fell on dead ears.

A scuffle broke out among the demons as more and more of them tried to suck energy from the crystal. Another broke out, and another. Shrieks and wails filled the air, and the number of demons grew so that it looked like a roiling blue cloud where they fought over the gem. Only the strong rays of the morning sun drove them away.

The master of the caravan, who had been waiting for mother Shiri to arrive, did not wait even for the morning sun.

As soon as the light grew bright enough to see, he ordered the nethik up and away from the flames of the many fires set around their camp. They were swiftly hitched to the wagons. Men and women scurried to break down tents and pack belongings; no one hunted and no one ate. The wagons were moving even before camp was fully broken, swiftly driving west and north along the trail that eventually would lead toward Ethkell. The caravan master intended to make at least two days distance from the camp in a single day. It would tax the nethik and everyone else who was traveling. But no one in the caravan objected, for the previous night, from the safety of huge fires, they had seen and heard the dance of the demons.

CHAPTER 17
Oumid is Sad

Although I am not usually sad, at this time I was sad because the elders from Tuklos came back and said that the men who had lost daughters and sisters and wives were not satisfied with the jewels from mother Shiri's chests. They wanted Al-Medi and the other leaders from Ak-Shamalim to pay with their lives. They had heard from the girls who survived about mother Shiri's training, and since mother Shiri was not there to shame or frighten the girls into silence, they talked to the elders and told them about the trainings and the bribes and the healing tents.

I found out that it was not the custom for the grehti to train the new wives in healing from mating. It was mother Shiri who had made it so that every girl had to do it. Since she was not there to threaten them, many of the girls who were bought complained to their husbands, and those men also wanted compensation from Ak-Shamalim. If mother Shiri had not accumulated such wealth, the other grehti of Ak-Shamalim would have been forced to pay. The other mothers had their wealth taken because they had been helping mother Shiri. Al-Medi said that he had not known the extent of the injuries of the women in the healing tents. The elders from Tuklos said that he should have known, and that he should have known the plans and behavior of his wife, therefore they took his wealth as well.

The talk in Ak-Shamalim was that the men of Tuklos were going to put Al-Medi to death at the hands of the reckoners.

The reckoners are from the Dekani tribe. Since they are considered unclean (but not as low as a nethik) they do all the unpleasant work of the Tuklos Rsakk. The reckoners are particularly cruel. They are called when attempts at resolution have failed and death is the only option. I had only heard of one thing they did; they caught a man who had been stealing knives from a Dekani dealer. The dealer had been told by the Tapestry Master to solve the problem himself.

The reckoners caught up to the man as he fled north; they brought him back in many pieces. They traveled back to Tuklos on foot. It was said that each morning and each night they cut a part from his body.

They delivered a chest of those parts to the merchant; on top of everything else was a heart still warm from the body of the thief.

Before the reckoners could arrive, the demons returned.

It was the sky that warned me before the alarm went out in Ak-Shamalim. It whispered "Danger!" to me, and sang to me of cold, and many demons. I looked over the edge of the cliff and saw the fires of a caravan burning high. This is a dangerous thing to do because bandits look for such things. It was curious to me and I thought I should talk to Al-Medi, but he was in his tent with a guard.

Morning came and went, and I still played and the sky sang and danced for me. I missed morning prayer, but still no one called for me. The song of the sky became urgent; it sang to me of hunger, conflict and death.

I thought that I must ask Al-Medi what these things meant, so I went to see him. The guards let me in and the guard inside rolled his eyes at me when I said it was important. Al-Medi was angry and sad at the same time. A guard stood inside the tent so I could not tell him what the sky had told me.

"My wife is missing," he said to me. "I had been thinking for a little time, that she did not love me as I loved her, and now it seems that I was right about that."

"You are a good leader," I said.

"No, Oumid, I am not. I might be a good person, but I am not a good leader. Many things have happened here that a good leader should know about, and I did not know about them. It is the nature of men to keep secrets from a leader if there are profits to be made from it. I knew that, and I did watch the people I thought were corrupt, but I did not suspect my wife."

"Maybe I should have swept out the tents and listened for you."

He laughed at that.

"That might have worked when they thought you were an ignorant nethik boy, but you are a warrior. Everyone knows you."

That surprised me and made me a little upset, because if people knew me they would come with requests. I thought about the mountains up north and wished I was there. I wished that Al-Medi could come, but I already knew that he would not like the cold.

I also knew that I should not offer to fly away somewhere else with him. He would not allow it; he would tell me that I would get in trouble, and that was true, so I did not offer.

Instead, I asked him who should I listen to and who should I go to with questions. That made him laugh again.

"Practical as usual, Oumid," he said. I did not mind that he said Oumid because it was the name he gave me.

He said that I should wait until there was someone who told me things to do that would not get me in trouble. He said that it might be good to go with Marai back to her tribe since I loved her.

I told Al-Medi that I probably did not love her. She did make feelings in me like the fire rising. He said that was enough.

He also said that her tribe lived in a place where the Mother's magic was not strong, and that I might not be able to shift.

"Will the sky be there?" I asked.

"It is the shape changing magic that is different. I'm sure they have winds and mountains, and the sky is blue there," said Al-Medi, but already I was worried because while they might have the sky, it might not be my sky. I could not think how to tell this to Al-Medi. Then the men came in to tell me that I was to have no more time with him. He hugged me as if I was still ten summers. Since I thought it would be the last time I would see him, I did not knock him down.

I stayed around those tents to see if there would be another chance to talk to Al-Medi. Instead, the k'g'hrah captain noticed me and put me on patrol. Since none of the rsakk wanted to fly with me they put me on the high patrol which was fine because my sight is good enough and I could visit the sky while I flew.

The alarm came just after evening prayer.

That was when my patrol was to begin; a k'g'hrah came back reporting that there were many, many demons in the area where the caravan had been. Some of the k'g'hrah who got closer had been attacked by speritu, but most of the demons were fighting amongst themselves. The k'g'hrah captain called me and told me that I should prove if I was invisible to speritu by going to watch them and find out what they were doing. I agreed since I wanted to look for Marai's sister.

As I flew down there I realized that since Al-Medi was no longer in charge of Ak-Shamalim, I might not need to kill the demon. I thought that I would follow it if I could.

There was no chance of that. There were too many to see one from another. The demons were fighting and shrieking and wailing, and hurting each other. There were so many that a blue glow lit the night. I saw something near them that looked like a nok or a rsakk; I thought that person must be dead, so I continued to watch.

I watched for a long time and still they did not notice me, and a lot of the demons had died or were hurt; they floated in the air and did not move.

When the daylight came the demons fled into the ground, and it was peaceful and quiet. I went back to the k'g'hrah captain and reported that there was a body out there. No one wanted to go out; they said it did not matter that the body of a caravan nok should rot in the sun. But I thought that Marai's demon might be there, so I went out. None of the demons on the ground looked like Marai's sister. While I was there I found and brought back the body of mother Shiri, her pack, and the box that was near her. There were pouches and a gem scattered on the sand, and I brought those as well.

The girls recognized one of the findings in the pack. It was made of tirothi twisted wire work. The finding was made to hold a gem shaped like a water drop; that was like one of the stones found in Tariq's possession, so they questioned him again.

Tariq admitted to stealing the gem from mother Shiri's chest; he had asked Chaipa to give it to him and she had refused. He saw mother Shiri give Chaipa the finding with another gem in it. After that was when the demons came.

By the time they finished talking to Tariq, Chaipa was awake. They took the gem in to show her and she became upset. Chaipa was something like the Tapestry Master's daughter, except among the tirothi it is called the Sender, and her father the Sender had given her the demon gem to take to Ak-Shamalim to be destroyed in the fires there. As was the custom, Chaipa's belongings were searched when she arrived at Ak-Shamalim. That was when mother Shiri had seen the gem. Mother Shiri had told Chaipa that she would have the gem destroyed by the grehti, and Chaipa believed her.

There was a legend among the tirothi about the gem, and when they heard about what happened at Merinell they decided that their gem should be destroyed. It was sent with Chaipa's entourage, but only Chaipa was allowed past the gates, so she took it with her.

The box was said to hold in the magic of the gem, so that it would not call demons. Marai was working in the healing tents and she told me how when the Tuklos elders heard that part of the story, they had panicked and put Chaipa's gem inside the box very quickly. It made me laugh the way she told it but I cannot tell it the same way.

They asked Chaipa to tell the legend and she told them the story called Demon Jewel. The elders from Tuklos had not heard it because it was a tirothi story. I will tell it to you but not as well as she told it because I am not tirothi.

CHAPTER 18
How a Tiroth Tells a Story

This is how a tiroth tells a story:

No one knows when, but everyone, each tirothi, every man and woman, knows that the jewel, the gem, the ugly one, was found in the trunk, the inside of the inside of a tree. The tirothi were skilled and crafty and dexterous, so they fashioned a box, a container, a thing to hold the gem made from the tree in which they had discovered and found it. This tree made wood that was very hard, tough and durable wood called hardwood, that was used for tools and knives and implements of all kinds. They did this to protect and honor and keep safe the jewel, for when they offered it to their Mother, who lived where all the trees are always reaching, growing –

that is near the sun in case you were unaware and did not know, yes, when they offered it to their Mother who lives with the sun, it became even more beautiful and it was almost too shiny and bright to look at. So they made, created and fashioned a box, a holder, a container for it that was carved and cut and shaped to be very beautiful and pretty. The explanation and reason for it was that the more beautiful the gem became, the more dangerous and deadly and hazardous it was. If it shone brightly enough then it would hurt and burn and kill anyone who touched it.

Now you know how the tirothi tell stories. I will tell the rest in the way of Kgh'jsh, which will not take from today into tomorrow, as Chaipa's telling went.

Each day the people did the offering, and each night they placed the gem at the foot of the Mother Tree, which is the tallest and widest in the jungle. This was done by the Sender, who brings bodies to the tree after death, so the souls can travel more quickly back to the Mother.

One day the Sender came to the village and told the people that demons had come to take the gem, and the gem had killed them. The people had been plagued by demons on occasion, but not since the gem had been placed under the tree. The gem was calling the demons and killing them so the people were safe. Because of this, only the elder who offered the gem to the Mother and the Sender who placed it by the Mother Tree were allowed to touch the box holding the gem. Because the gem was inside a box made of the wood of the tree where they found it, the gem was called the hidden gem.

At that time the tirothi had just begun to do trade with others. This came about because of the visit of the grehti, who came to them and showed them how to control the time of the change.

It happened back then that one day there came to the village of the hidden gem some men who said they could help the people of the village when the wild time came. The wild time came at skydark and sometimes at other times, and at that time some of the people would change into animals. The animals had long, agile arms and could run around in the trees. So at that time the people, who lived on platforms, built huts on the ground made from strong wood for both walls and roof. In these huts they would hide and defend themselves. Some of the animals ran into the jungle, but others came to attack the people with claws and poison fangs. Some would die because the animals would bite many times, and if there were too many bites the breathing would stop and the people would die.

The huts were made of hard wood, the animals could not bite through it, and it was the same wood as from the tree in which the gem was found. It is said that this was how the gem was found, when men were cutting wood to make huts to be safe from the animals.

The men who came said that the animals could be changed back into men, and have control over the change. There was an objection because the people who could not change said that the people who could change would have the advantage and kill them.

So the men who came, who called themselves grehti, said that all the people could change, and they would teach them how. Each time at skydark, when the mother's magic was greatest, they would show a few more people how to change, and soon it came to pass that only the oldest and some of the sick were unable to change. These people were defended by the people who could change.

It also came to pass that some of the wild ones learned to change back into men by seeing how the others changed. The grehti were happy to learn this because it made showing people how to change much easier. This is how the tirothi taught the grehti something about shapefinding.

The grehti promised to return to the village at each skydark because it required mind powers to show people how to change. They also traded with the tirothi. When they left they took with them some of the tirothi, who were to learn how to touch the mind and teach the shift. They left a grehti behind to teach people more about how to control the shift.

Some other people went with the ones who left and followed the grehti group to a place called Ethkell. There was a river there that was shallow and could be crossed without much danger. Boats landed there from other places. There were people there who also could change into animals, but they had different shapes, bird and taralk and lizard. The grehti and their students continued on their way; they were going to a place called Eileah.

The tirothi who had gone with them to Ethkell went back to the tirothi village and reported all they had seen. Many tirothi went down that trail to see what they could trade with the people at Ethkell; they wanted the shiny metal tools and cloth and the other things that had been told to them. The tirothi were skilled at making things of wood and at wood carving, but their tools had been wood and bone and stone. They wanted metal knives to make better designs in the wood. They wanted the cloth because they thought it was pretty; they never had seen such colors as in the nethik dyes. Their own clothing was woven from fibers they found; they did not know how to make dyes so everything was the same color.

So the tirothi came down from their trees and traded for metal and cloth. This was the beginning of trade for the tirothi. Because of it, the trail to the tirothi village was made wider and became a road. And some of the people from Ethkell began to go to the tirothi village to see what was there and to trade with them. It could not be prevented that someone would be in the village and see the ritual of the hidden jewel.

No one in Ethkell had seen such a thing, and some of them wanted the gem. The tirothi elder said the gem was sacred and not to be traded. This caused some conflict among the tirothi, but because they had other things to trade they left the gem where it was, until a man came from Ethkell who said that he would convince the tirothi to give him the gem.

His name was Hskail, and he stayed in the tirothi village for a while making offers to the elder, and each time the elder said no.

The first time the trader went to Ethkell and returned with a cart of taralk meat.

"No," said the elder, "That meat smells of death; it will remind my people of the wild times when people ate people. I do not want my people to think of those times. We eat from the trees, and we are content."

The trader took the meat back. He had to throw it into the river because by the time he got back to Ethkell it was spoiled and no one would trade for it.

Then the trader returned with stone carvings from the north. The cart was very heavy and required a number of taralk to pull it. The carvings were pretty and shiny; they were carved from a smooth rock and had veins of a substance that sparkled in the sun. The people from the tirothi village crowded around the cart and wanted to touch the carvings.

The elder said, "No, those will make our platforms too heavy, and everything will fall to the ground."

The people did not want that to happen so they refused to trade with Hskail for the smooth stone carvings. The trader grumbled and went away, but very soon he returned with another cart. This time it was filled with very fine cloth in many colors. The colors were very beautiful and the people all exclaimed and talked and touched the cloth.

The elder was very smart. He said to the trader, "There is not enough here to compensate for the stone. Besides, we do not need cloth, it is always warm here."

He made the people put back the cloth. They grumbled and complained and said things against the elder, but they did it.

The trader was angry; he had traded everything he had for the cart of cloth. The tirothi elder said that he would consider trading the gem for two or three carts of cloth. He thought this would make the trader go away. He did not want to trade the gem for anything.

The trader said that he would bring something much more beautiful and useful than the cloth, so they should make ready to trade for it. Then the elder thought that the trader would bring something even more valuable than three carts of cloth, so he agreed to come and look and consider it when the trader returned.

The trader told the elder that he would return with something so valuable that guards would be needed to ensure its safety. He told the elder that he should make sure to keep the gem safe in case any thieves should hear of the trade and decide to take the sacred stone.

The elder did not intend to trade the stone for anything the trader brought, but the trader's words made him worry about its safety. So he ordered the gem to be brought from its hiding place near the Mother Tree, and the Sender went into the jungle to get it. The elder said that the Sender should show the stone to the departed ones one last time, and then bring it to the elder.

The trader had gone only a little way into the woods. He waited for the Sender to go into the jungle and followed him to the Mother Tree. He waited and watched while the Sender brought out the jewel from its hiding place, and laid it at the foot of the Mother Tree. When night came, the trader made certain that the Sender was asleep, and then he tried to steal it.

The Sender was asleep on his platform, which was in a tree near the Mother Tree; this was the safest place to be when the demons came to be killed by the stone. That night there was a commotion near the stone and the Sender heard screams. He thought the screams were the demons, so he covered his ears and said prayers to the Mother. Soon all was quiet and he went back to sleep.

The next morning he discovered Hskail dead under the tree. The trader was both burned and frozen; by this the Sender knew that Hskail had touched the stone and that the demons had taken the rest of his life.

Hskail was not tirothi so they sent his body out of the jungle to Ethkell with a message to the elder of Ethkell about what had happened and that they should dispose of the body because of the demons.

After hearing the story the elders at Ethkell said that the stone should be left to the tirothi; that it should be left alone. No one who saw the body of the trader wanted to suffer his fate.

The grehti heard of the story and went to see the stone, but the elder of the tirothi brought them to a great and deep ravine, and said they had thrown it in there since it had killed someone. The grehti went away, and some summers later, the rsakk came to Ethkell. There the tirothi traded with the rsakk, who gave them shiny rocks. The tirothi remembered the hidden gem and carved the rocks into shapes that were like the hidden gem.

When the rsakk came back with more rocks the tirothi went to meet them and showed them the carved stones. This was the beginning of the trade of gems between the tirothi and the rsakk.

This is where the tirothi legend ends. Chaipa told them a little bit more so that the elders and the grehti could understand how the gem had come to Ak-Shamalim.

She said that the stone had been buried near the Mother Tree, and the Sender was instructed that no one should find it. It came to pass that the Sender came to the elders and told them that demons were attracted to the Mother Tree and were not killed by the stone beneath it. The stone was calling them, but it was too weak to kill them because the ritual of the hidden jewel had been forgotten. It had not been kept since the time of Hskail. They thought that another trader might come to steal it, and then the grehti and the people of Ethkell would come with weapons and kill the tirothi people. Now many years had passed and the stone was calling the demons but not killing them. There was concern that the demons would come into the tirothi towns and kill the people.

So the Sender dug up the stone and brought it to the elders, who decided that it should be destroyed. They did not want harm to come to the carrier so they made a new box of the wood from the same kind of tree as the one where the stone was discovered. They sent it with the Sender's daughter, and she was to present it to the grehti of Ak-Shamalim to be thrown into the great fire as an offering. They thought that it could be destroyed by the fires at Ak-Shamalim, which are kept very hot.

But mother Shiri had taken the box with the gem. Chaipa objected and told the story, and mother Shiri said that she would take it and make spells to make sure it was destroyed, and that Chaipa should make a different offering. Chaipa did not know that the gem had been kept, because she trusted mother Shiri.

CHAPTER 19
The Reckoners

Chaipa asked them to destroy the jewel since mother
Shiri had not destroyed it as promised.

When the elders heard Chaipa's stories they went to
the tent where Al-Medi was and let him out. He was not
to be the head of Ak-Shamalim anymore because he
should have had more control over what was happening
in the women's tents – not the training, but all the jewels
that were there. They allowed him to keep some of his
wealth since mother Shiri's wealth had paid for the losses
at Ak-Shamalim. Al-Medi also owned a caravan, and he
said that he would go and live in the caravan. A number
of the girls were not spoken for and Al-Medi sent to
their fathers for permission because they had served well

in his tents. He asked for Oumid to go with him but his caravan would be on the ground and Kgh'jsh needed to be in a high place for the wind and the sky.

"I understand, Oumid," he said, and made me promise to come and talk to him and ask him for advice. I said that I would. I was very happy that I would not have to look for another person to talk to and to ask questions.

He was made to leave quickly, which made me sad. They gave him only a few days to gather his possessions and organize his house to move to the caravan. He told me his caravan's route: it went from the mines in the east to Tuklos, then to Ak-Shamalim and then around the north side of the forbidden forest, ending at Eileah. I had decided to go north, back to the mountains around Tollach or Cnieren. Those were north and east of his route, so I knew that I would not see him often.

I went up to the cliffs to play my flute and listen to the sky, and not even a good climber like Marai could find me. That was a mistake because when I came down to say goodbye to Al-Medi, Marai was gone.

The Tuklos elders had examined her and determined that she should be trained at Eileah. They thought that if the demons were trying to harm her that she should be well trained and that there would be more protection at Eileah. I thought that she must have tried to find me because when I went to the cave that we shared, my clothing was laid out and there was a gift wrapped in cloth on my sleeping cloth.

The cloth was of a kind I had not seen before; it was like the finest of nethik cloth. Inside, there was a short length of string, and on the string there was a bead made of a shiny stone. I looked close at the string and I saw that it was woven from hair, and it was red like hers. The string hung all the way down into my tunic. I wondered what would happen to it when I shifted.

I showed it to Al-Medi, and he said it meant that I was to wait for her. I asked him why I should wait for her when she did not wait for me, and he laughed and said I should ask her, but that I should be ready to duck when I asked.

Al-Medi had a gift for me too; it was a tiny shield. It was made like the shield of a rsakk warrior, with eyes that looked at me and teeth painted around the edges. It was painted in colors I did not know, and Al-Medi said that they were the colors of his tribe. He told me that like Marai, he was from a desert tribe, but not so far away as hers. He said that if I got into trouble that I should show the shield to all the rsakk I met, and help would come to me. He said that if I were to lose the shield that I should say that I had been adopted into the tribe of Akhad Rai. If the rsakk looked at the shield, or heard the name Akhad Rai, and held up their hand and said, "Brother," then I should do the same. Then they would take hold of my arm to greet me, which was the greeting of the people of Akhad Rai. If they did not hold up their hand and say, "Brother," then I should not speak to them of my trouble.

I had heard that Akhad Rai was a powerful merchant whose caravans are more like towns than caravans. I wondered why Al-Medi had not called for help when they said he was to die, and he said that if the order had been given, that Akhad Rai would have come to help him.

I was not sure how this could happen, but the day Al-Medi was to leave, I found out.

On that day, a group of men met us at the gate. I had gone with Al-Medi and his women and the nethik servants to help and so that I would know his caravan if I saw it from the air. The men who met us were from Tuklos, and they demanded more of Al-Medi's wealth for their women. These were not the women who went with us, they were the women who had died.

The men had brought warriors with them. The warriors pointed spears at us and would not let us go on our way.

Al-Medi said no, that they had been compensated and the elders were satisfied. The men said that they had hired the reckoners to put things right; if Al-Medi did not give them all the wealth of his caravan, and the women besides, they would give him to the reckoners.

Al-Medi laughed and said, let them try.

They held us there, outside the gates of Ak-Shamalim, and no one came to help because we were no longer of Ak-Shamalim. Al-Medi told me not to shift because if I did they would kill me with their spears.

Soon in the distance we saw dust, and the women cried because it was the reckoners. They said they would rather go with the men back to Tuklos. Al-Medi told them to stand with him, and because he had been kind to them they did.

The reckoners were in shape, they were almost all of them red rsakk which are said to be the most fierce and dangerous. I wondered if it would hurt badly when they cut pieces off me. I was worried that they would cut the string Marai had given me, which I was wearing around my neck.

The reckoners shifted back to nok and surrounded us, pointing spears at us. They were wearing the reckoner clothes, which are tunics with no decoration or embroidery. One of them asked the Tuklos men if we were the ones they were supposed to take. The Tuklos men said yes.

But at that moment Al-Medi showed them the little shield he had that was just like the one he had given me. He tied it to his robe, and all the women and nethik servants did the same with shields that he had given them. I tied mine to my robe as well. When I did I hoped that Al-Medi would not be angry with me. I should have asked him about what I did.

Al-Medi said that the men from Tuklos were looking for money and that they had been paid their bride prices, but the men from Tuklos said that they had not been paid the full price.

The reckoners said that they would hear the stories of both sides, and then they would decide.

WOLF TINKER AND JOANNA ERBACH

Al-Medi asked the reckoners if I could go free, because I was only making sure that his family got out of Ak-Shamalim. They said yes, and Al-Medi told me to fly south and west and I would find the tents of Akhad Rai. But I stayed there with Al-Medi, and told him that Akhad Rai would come to help him. It was then that Al-Medi told me that Akhad Rai did not have magic; the trick was to send me to the tents of Akhad Rai, and then Akhad Rai would send help. Al-Medi said that the reckoners would respect the shield of Rai and listen to him. Meanwhile I was to go to the tents of Akhad Rai for help.

"I cannot," I told him.

"You must, Oumid," said Al-Medi, "Our lives depend on it."

"I cannot," I told him, because I could not, because I had done something without asking him.

Al-Medi sighed.

"Why can't you go, Oumid?"

"I cannot say."

"You don't know why you can't go?"

"I know why."

"Why can't you go?"

"Because I cannot."

"Oumid, I am not asking you, I am telling you to go."

"I cannot," I said, and a reckoner came to us because he saw that we were talking, and our voices had become loud.

The reckoner said that if I did not want to go, then I would have to stay and be killed, which made sense to me. Al-Medi looked angry but did not hit me on the back of the head. I was glad of that, because I was tired.

In the next moments, more reckoners arrived. There was confusion because the reckoners that were already there had not called for any more reckoners. There were ten of the new ones, and they shifted to nok and held spears, but the spears were pointed at the Tuklos reckoners. When the new reckoners shifted I saw that they were wearing something on their tunics.

They were wearing the shields of Akhad Rai!

Al-Medi grinned at the men from Tuklos and said, "I think now we will have a talk."

The reckoners from Tuklos laid down their spears and while they all talked together the leader of Akhad's reckoners came over to us. Al-Medi went with his hand held up in greeting, but the leader of Akhad's reckoners came over to me and took hold of my arm, because that is the greeting of the men from the caravan of Akhad Rai.

He said, "Brother," to me, and I answered, "Brother," and behind us Al-Medi was making odd noises. I looked around and he was making the noises one makes when something is too hot to eat.

"H – h – h," he said, and finally he said, "How?"

I bowed my head in front of him and said, "I am very sorry, I did something without asking."

"What?" he said, and I told him how I had heard the men of Tuklos saying that they would call the reckoners to avenge their daughters. So it was that on the nights I flew patrol I went from caravan to caravan and found the one that belonged to Akhad Rai. I showed them the shield and told them my trouble, and they said help would come, and that I should say nothing to anyone but wait with Al-Medi.

"That is why I could not go," I said to Al-Medi.

"And why could you not tell me?"

"They said I should not tell anyone. They did not say I should tell you."

Al-Medi sighed.

"I shall have to tell them about you," he said. He was smiling when he said it.

Then Al-Medi laughed and held out his arm to the leader of Akhad's reckoners, who took hold of it, and they said to each other, "Brother." And then Al-Medi took hold of my arm and said to me, "Brother," so I said "Brother" back to him. That gave me a good feeling inside that I cannot describe because it was unfamiliar to me.

When they saw how many reckoners were there from Akhad Rai's caravan, the men from Tuklos said that they were satisfied, and left. Al-Medi tried to pay the reckoners from Tuklos and apologized for the false contract. They refused his payment. They said that the men from Tuklos were going to pay them three times that amount, and more. At that time I thought that I was glad I was not one of the men from Tuklos.

CHAPTER 20
The Merchant's Caravan

I had gone to the caravan of Akhad Rai. I was afraid to do it because I thought that they would not know me and kill me. I did not think they would wait to look at the shield that Al-Medi had given me.

Still, I could not stay at Ak-Shamalim after I heard the men grumbling about Al-Medi and saying he should be punished.

The grehti took all the wealth of mother Shiri and the other mothers and paid the men who had lost daughters and wives, but some of the men were not satisfied. I was there when they were paid, and when the grehti were done and went away, the men began to talk.

They talked near me as if I was sweeping the tents, and they said that they should have been paid more.

Some of the men were satisfied, and they said, "We should be happy that we have been given the bride price; our daughters could have been eaten by worms or died from the training."

Another man said, "Yes, that has happened before."

There was a man there wearing Vahtani robes. He said, "We have lost any profits we might have made from a higher bride price if the girls had been talented in one way or another. What if they had been found to have grehti skills?"

"They were tested before now," said another. "I do not think anything would have changed."

"Al-Medi is responsible. He should pay," said the Vahtani man. "The grehti should persuade him. He has a caravan. He is still wealthy."

"It will not happen," said another man who was wearing Esgeni robes. "The grehti rarely change a decision."

"Then we should persuade Al-Medi to consider giving us a part of his wealth. Some of those girls were being trained in his tents."

"That is not where they died," said another Vahtani man. "We may not be successful. Al-Medi is fair."

"Al-Medi is no longer the head of Ak-Shamalim," said the first Vahtani man. "He will leave Ak-Shamalim, and that is when we should persuade him."

"But," said the Esgeni man, "his caravan is connected with the caravan of Akhad Rai. That man will come to defend him."

"No," said the first Vahtani man, "Al-Medi is proud. He thinks that he is fair and that he is a good leader. He will not call for Akhad Rai unless he learns of some danger."

"I will not be part of this," said the Esgeni man, and he called his people and they left.

The first Vahtani man said, "I will call the reckoners to persuade him. I will tell them that Al-Medi refused us compensation for our losses."

The other Vahtani man agreed, and several others did as well, saying that the cost of the reckoners could be had from Al-Medi once he was persuaded to pay them. I heard them agree to approach him on the day that Al-Medi left Ak-Shamalim. Once he was away from the gates, there was a chance that he could shift and run away. But because the gate is in a narrow place, they could confront him without trouble.

I thought about telling Al-Medi, but I thought that if I did that, the men would change their plan to one I did not know about. It was a difficult time for me because I could not ask Al-Medi what to do without telling him the plan. So I thought about what Al-Medi would tell me to do if I asked him, and I thought that he would tell me to go to the caravan of Akhad Rai and get help.

If they confronted him at the gate he would not have time to go to the caravan of Akhad Rai. Since I was not confined to Ak-Shamalim, I thought that Al-Medi would tell me to go to the caravan of Akhad Rai before the day that Al-Medi was to leave Ak-Shamalim.

I flew looking for the caravan at night. I did my patrols, but when it was time for me to be finished, I flew into the desert and along the roads to find caravans. Before this I had not known how many there were. I went to three caravans; the third one was the one of Akhad Rai. The location of it was told to me by the people in the second caravan. They warned me that if I was a trader, or if I planned some harm, that it would not go well. I did not mean any harm so I thought that they might let me live until I showed them the shield.

The caravan was very big; there were more wagons than I could count. The camp was as big as some of the little villages north of the forbidden forest. I flew near the caravan and three k'g'hrah flew near me and asked me what I was doing there. I told them that I was in trouble and looking for Akhad Rai and they told me to land and shift back to nok.

When I shifted a large number of rsakk in shape surrounded me. I had hung the shield around my neck and I showed it to them. They shifted to nok and looked at the shield, and after that they smiled at me and held their hands up and said, "Brother."

We had landed a short distance from the caravan, so we walked to the gate. The gate was formed from wagons set together like a wall. There was an opening, and in front of the opening, there were guards both in nok and in shape. The men who were with me spoke to the nok guards and they let us in.

From the air, the caravan looked like a village, and the place where they took me was like the center of the village. It was enclosed in another wall of wagons and tents, and there were women cooking and children playing and men sitting in groups talking. It was noisy, but the fires were well fed and tended. The men were at ease; they drank ruka and laughed and told stories.

We went past men and the women and children, and no one looked at me or was alarmed. I thought that was strange since there had been speritu attacks, and since the elders from Tuklos had issued an alarm to everyone in the area.

They made me go into a tent where there was a man there who was not many summers from shapehouse. I thought that he must be a servant and this the tent of Akhad Rai because the tent was very fine and cushions were laid all around. The tent had a fire inside a pot instead of on the ground, like the ones in the grehti tents, and over the pot there was spiced meat cooking. The servant was turning the mcat, so I was surprised when he held up his hand and said, "Brother," because that is not what servants are supposed to do. Since he had done it I held up my hand and said, "Brother."

He stood up then, and I saw that he was not wearing the clothes of a servant. He told me to sit on the cushions but I was uncomfortable because I was used to solid ground. The man laughed and he told me that it was allowed to sit on the ground.

He gave me some ruka to drink and he said that he was Akhad Rai. I was confused, because of the stories. I thought he would be a big man, like me, and have a crest braided into his hair like a warrior, and have women serving him and cooking for him.

He was the size of most rsakk men, and his hair was not braided and there were no women in the tent. He was cooking his own food.

He looked at the shield and asked me about Al-Medi. I told him what I had heard. He said that he would send help, and he clapped his hands and said, "Shan." A man appeared in the tent so quickly that I thought it must be a spell.

"Al-Medi needs help," he said to the man. "It seems that what we have been hearing is true." Shan sat down and Akhad Rai gave him a cup of ruka. Then Akhad Rai asked me to say again what I had heard, and then he asked me about myself, and why I had come.

I told him that I had thought about what Al-Medi might tell me to do, and I had done that.

He said that I had done a good thing, and that he would send help. I was not to tell anyone that I had come there or that help would come.

I did not understand.

Akhad Rai was kind, like Al-Medi. He explained to me that if anyone knew that help was coming, men from Tuklos could find out and then they would change their plan and attack Al-Medi at a time when help could not be sent.

So I went back to Ak-Shamalim as if I had been on patrol, and told no one where I had been or that I had met Akhad Rai.

Al-Medi was glad that I had done it; the men from Tuklos were gone and would not harm him, and so I went with him to his caravan and saw them leave; then I went back to Ak-Shamalim because I still had patrols.

CHAPTER 21
The Voice of the Wind

Ak-Shamalim was a bad place without Al-Medi. There was no one to explain things to me. The new grehti were busy. Most of the k'g'hrah and all of the mothers were new. There was Garad-grah, and there was Shavadi-rsakk, but I did not like them the way I liked Al-Medi. After a time I left Ak-Shamalim and went to Eileah. There are high mountains there, and the sky was blue but the wind was not as friendly. I played my flute anyway, and the sky came and sang and danced as it had at Ak-Shamalim.

A k'g'hrah came to where I was and asked what I was doing there. I knew him and he knew me so we talked.

"There is a woman at Eileah," I said. "I think by now she is sixteen summers. I am going to pay her bride price and take her to my cave."

"You are k'g'hrah," he said. "K'g'hrah do not pay bride price."

"I am from Ak-Shamalim. I will pay her bride price."

"Which woman?"

"The one named Marai."

His face became very serious and he said, "She is grehti. It is unlikely that she will accept."

"She? Where is her father?"

"That would be High Grehti Cailtoh. He would not accept her bride price from you because he wants her for himself."

"Ah," I said, and we stood like that for a little while.

"When will she become his wife?" I asked.

"She will not," said the k'g'hrah.

"Ah," I said, and we stood like that a little while longer.

After a time, I began to play my flute.

"I must return to my patrol," said the patrol k'g'hrah.

"I will return to my mountain after I have played my flute for a little while," I said to him.

"I will tell the grehti," he said, and he flew away.

Later, I flew to Eileah at a time when there were many people outside. Soon a k'g'hrah flew alongside me and asked me what I was doing there.

"I want to see a woman before I go back to my mountain," I said. "I want to see the one named Marai."

"I will fly with you until you see her," he said.

He flew alongside me until I saw her. He did not need to show me which one was Marai because she was not wearing a hat or a hood. She was wearing a grehti robe; it was red, and matched her hair.

She did not see me.

Then I flew back toward Cnieren, and the k'g'hrah who had been following me flew back to Eileah.

I thought about how Marai might be looking for me, or maybe she was not. There were other things to do, so I did them. There was the sky to sing, good weather for flying and places to hunt taralk.

The spider mites were bad that summer. I had to sweep out my cave many times, and I had to burn my furs because some of the spider mites lived after I picked them out. They found my furs and made them a sticky mess. After the furs burned the cave smelled bad, so I went down to the nethik village and stayed there for a while; they gave me food to eat while I waited for the smell to leave my cave. I could have gone to Cnieren, but I did not want to trade or dig ore, and that is what is done there. So I went to the nethik village, where I learned many things. In the nethik village they hunt in nok shape; I went with them and learned how to hunt taralk and stripefur and other small things. If I hunted in the morning I could eat what I caught, but if I hunted during the day I should bring some back for the children and the sick. The nethik do not leave their sick even though they do not heal swiftly like rsakk. The women used the meat I brought to make porridge, which is easy to eat in nok shape. I ate some too, and it was good, so many times I hunted extra meat even after I was full. The women in the village liked me for that reason.

When I went back to my cave it was empty and clean; someone had come and taken all my things. I remembered Marai then, and thought how if she had been in my cave the spider mites would not have eaten my furs and if anyone had come to take my things she would have slapped them with her fist.

I had carried my flute down to the village, and my clothes, and the string made from Marai's hair, as well as the jewels and the shield Al-Medi had given me. My food and sleeping cloth and my water pouch were gone, so I had to go back down to the village and trade for more. It was another day before I came back to my camp, and then it rained so I had to sit inside to play my flute. The sky came but she sang a sad song.

I stayed in my camp for many days after that. The sky was a good companion. I hunted and played my flute for the sky and sometimes when the sun was setting I watched the blue night overtake the sun, but only after there was a fire in the sky. The fire made me think of Marai, of her hair, and the fire dance. She was grehti now, and priests do not clean caves or pick spider mites.

Around that time of day the sky would dance for me. To know those steps she must have watched the dancers as Marai had. In those times I did not miss Marai so much.

One day a strange thing happened when I played my flute and spoke to the sky about Marai. The sky whispered to me in the voice of the wind. It said that I should go find her. I knew where she was, at Eileah over the mountains, and I showed the sky which way that was.

It was quiet after that. The sky did not dance and sing. She did not speak to me. There were only small breezes. I thought the sky must have gone to Eileah to look for Marai.

So I thought I would go to Eileah again.

When I went, they knew me. The k'g'hrah who met me as I flew there asked my name, and when I told him, he said I should land so they could talk to me. The ones who wanted to talk to me were elders there. I knew this was a great honor but I had not brought my prayer clothes with me. I was very surprised when they gave me some clothes and invited me to eat a meal.

I asked where Marai was and they said she was gone.

That meant that I should leave, but they said I should stay. They asked me questions about when I met Marai, but the only thing I remembered was that Al-Medi had said to say nothing.

So I did not tell them about all the things that happened at Ak-Shamalim. There was one of the elders there who tried to touch my mind, but after a while he began making the same groaning noises the mothers made when I did something wrong. When I asked if I had done something wrong, they said no.

Then they asked me questions about seeing demons. I could not see them any better than anyone else. I had heard them better. The elders were interested in this and they asked if I could hear any demons in the room where they were talking to me and I said no. That caused them to talk a lot and they asked me if I knew the difference between the truth and a lie, and because Al-Medi had taught me that, I said yes.

They asked if I had seen a demon at Ak-Shamalim, and I said yes, I had seen many. They asked if I had seen Marai call a demon, and I said no. They asked if I had seen a demon following her and I said no about that too. The demon that attacked us had not been following us. They did not ask about that so I did not tell them.

They looked into my mind again after that, but they told me that they were going to do it, which was different from the grehti at Ak-Shamalim. I asked if they were going to make me shapebound, and they laughed and said no, unless I had done something bad, and since I had not done anything bad I felt better.

They kept looking into my mind until I got a headache, and I told them, and they said things like, "He must not know," and, "Why did no one tell him?" and that made me curious because I thought I knew what I was thinking.

They told me then that it had been two summers and not one since Marai had gone to Eileah.

They told me that Marai had gone back to her desert tribe because a demon kept attacking her. She had learned almost everything a grehti could learn, so they had sent her back early. At that moment I realized that I should have sent word to her about where I was so that she could have visited me or asked me to visit her. I could have gone with her to protect her from the demon. They said that as a grehti she would know how to protect herself until she got back to her tribe.

When I asked them how her tribe would protect her, they said that her tribe lived in a place where the demons did not like to go. I thought it must be a place where they keep fires burning all night like at Ak-Shamalim. But the demons had gone there too. So her tribe must be somewhere else.

They told me that she was going in a caravan to her tribe, but they could not tell me anything more than that the caravan had left perhaps two moons ago.

Again I thought that I should have invited her to my mountain. She had liked the view from the cliffs at Ak-Shamalim. She might have liked the view from the cliffs northwest of Cnieren.

She was rsakk, so I thought that I could go to the caravan and see her, and maybe she would come back with me for a little while before she went to her tribe. I could protect her from the demons. I had done it before.

CHAPTER 22
Finding Marai

I went to look for the caravan that carried Marai. It was the warm season so there were many, even going from Eileah and Cnieren. After a few caravans I was lucky to find the caravan of Al-Medi. But Al-Medi was not there. I learned that he had gone to join the caravans of Akhad Rai, because while he was in his own caravan an attempt was made to kill him. They thought the assassins were from the grehti because of what happened at Ak-Shamalim, but some of them said that it was because the grehti did not want the stories and secrets of Ak-Shamalim to be told by Al-Medi.

Al-Medi had gone to join Akhad Rai's caravan but disappeared before he reached it. That was all they could tell me. This made me sad, because it seemed to me that he must be dead. If they did not succeed in killing him with assassins, then they would send the reckoners, and if Al-Medi was not in the caravan of Akhad Rai, they would kill him. The reckoners would listen to him if it were a dispute, but the reckoners used by the grehti listen to no one.

After more searching I found the caravan that carried Marai; it was the smallest one I had seen. Since all of them were rsakk it seemed it would be safe from bandits, but I went along with them because I wanted to protect her and also I wanted to see her tribe.

When Marai saw me she smiled and talked to me about what happened at Eileah. She said that her demon had come and attacked her. It had not attacked anyone else at Eileah, so at first they thought that she was calling it with some magic unknown to them. But after they looked into her mind they saw that she was not calling the demon. They did find out that the demon had been her sister, but they were unable to destroy it because it ran away whenever anyone else came near. This was unlike most demons, which continue to attack even when they are being killed.

So they decided that Marai could not stay at Eileah. Her tribe did not have a grehti so she was needed for that reason as well. I asked her how she would be an elder since she was a woman and should only be having babies. For this Marai slapped my head. Even though it hurt I liked it. She said that she was not made to have children.

The demon had not come to the caravan that was carrying her, so they thought that maybe it did not know she had left Eileah and was still there looking for her. I thought that it might come to the caravan so I asked if I could go with them to protect her. The grehti laughed but they let me come.

It was a long journey in nok or even in shape, and I offered to carry her there but they said it could not be done. Only High Grehti Cailtoh could bring her there. Cailtoh-rsakk said he was her mate, but Marai told me that she would not mate with him. I wondered if she had slapped him with her fist when he tried to mate with her.

Although it was a long journey I did not see much of Marai because of Cailtoh-rsakk; he always had some errand for me and at other times he was together in the wagon with Marai. The nethik slaves pulling the wagons said that he was supposed to be teaching her the things a grehti needs to know, but they said that many times he also was trying to convince her to mate with him.

At last wc came to the end of the journey, which to my surprise was Ak-Shamalim. I was told that from there High Grehti Cailtoh would take her. I could not go because they were going to travel in ways only known to the grehti. It was alright with me. Marai could pick spider mites and make my cave comfortable, but I did not want her enough to lose my sky. If there is such a thing as love, that makes people mate for life as the tirothi do, then I love the sky. I thought that if I showed her, that Marai would love the sky too.

She was sad when I told her, but she said that there was a rsakk in her tribe who she loved, and that she and I could be friends. That was alright with me so I gave her the gift I had prepared, a picture to show her my sky, since she had not been able to come to my mountain to see it dance. I told her that it should remind her of me. She said that she would remember me by it and that made me glad.

I spent the night at Ak-Shamalim because I wanted to see Marai leave, and because I thought that Al-Medi's caravan might be near there. When I awoke in the morning she was gone; they had gone in the middle of the night.

I was sad about not finding Al-Medi because he told me useful things and I had not found anyone kind enough to do that. There is the nethik elder Nishom, in the village below Cnieren, but he is nethik and so he does not know some of the things of rsakk and k'g'hrah.

This is the end of my story; I have told you all that I know. Until you came to my mountain, I was there playing my flute and watching the sky dance.

What was the gift? I can show you if you like. Give me a bit of skin and paints and a brush and I will show it to you.

CHAPTER 23
Dekan

Marai sat alone in the common room of the Canny Farmhouse in Dekan. She was both dismayed and comforted to know that things had not changed much since she'd left. Her childhood friends had gone off to sea, or to work in the city, or to more mundane jobs in Dekan.

She hadn't kept track of what happened to the boy who went with her to Karn. Likely he'd stayed. Marai had wanted to stay. The minute she'd gone through the portal back to Dekan, she'd felt it: a loss, a familiarity gone from the air. She hadn't tried to change her shape in Dekan. She knew it would be harder. There was less of it here – less magic. There wasn't a better word for it.

Did she miss the odd keegrah man who had been a strange mix of hard to find and good company? She missed Mirabel. She'd wanted to stay for Bel as well. Mirabel her sister, her twin, who had gone everywhere and done everything with her. Mirabel had stayed on Karn. She'd been transformed into something that they called a demon.

Marai didn't believe in demons. Still, the rest of the grehti magic worked, so it was reasonable to assume that the rules that governed her sister's change into that form, whatever it was, would provide an answer to bringing Mirabel back. It was magic, and magic could be studied and used.

Marai rubbed her eyes. She'd gone to Tapolith and had gotten the best books on magic. Al-Medi's gifts had come in handy; it turned out that gems on Karn were the same as gems in Tapolith. She'd come back with wealth.

It didn't make up for losing her sister.

Marai yawned and rubbed her eyes again. Bel wasn't going to take over the Canny household now, and Ma Canny was putting a lot of pressure on Marai to take the job. She told herself that it wouldn't be as bad as she'd thought. She wasn't going to let anybody call her "Ma," though. She'd think of something else. At the Canny farm she'd be close to the portal – if she learned something that might help Bel, she could go back to Karn and try it.

Marai had been home for a quarter moon. Karn life was fading as Dekan life reasserted itself. There were not many people who returned to Dekan from a successful shapefinding. She'd find out who the others were. They shared something.

Something –

Suddenly she remembered the dirty bit of skin Oumid had given her. She had not unwrapped his gift. She winced – even in her memory, he was as invisible as he had been on Karn. She went up to her sleeping stall, where her things were as she had left them when she arrived home. She'd gotten the pack and the clothing on Karn, and touching them reminded her of Bel. Shrugging off sadness, she dug around in the pack until she found it.

It was a dirty piece of skin folded several times over a hard object. The object was a bone whistle. Marai smiled. She should have expected as much – he loved the sky so. It would, as he hoped, remind her of the sky and the wind. But what had he meant by "gifts?" There was only one whistle in the package.

The candle light flickered and a bit of color caught her eye. The wrapping – it wasn't dirt – he had painted something on it. A picture of the sky?

She smoothed it out. A gasp escaped her throat.

It was a painting, made with nethik dyes. The nethik had taught him more than just how to hunt.

It was indeed a picture of the sky, and now she understood what he meant when he said that he had fallen in love with the sky.

The flicker of hope she'd been nursing for three years burst into flames.

The picture, done in blue and black dyes, was a portrait of her sister – not in pain or in fear, but with joy lighting her face. In the background, there was a figure of a man sitting on the edge of a cliff, playing a flute. Oumid, who loved his flute, who loved the sky, was playing for her sister. Tears welled up and Marai closed her eyes, but still she could see it, and if she listened she could hear it, the haunting sounds of the flute playing the melody of the fire dance, and her sister, Bel, twirling and dancing the steps close to him, not dead, not demon, but alive.

CHAPTER 24
Al-Medi Is Not Here

Oumid had been sent to another tent. Meanwhile, the shashigai sat musing over the picture Oumid had drawn for him. The woman in the picture was clearly what they called a demon, yet this was what Oumid called the sky, the one who spoke to him. The girl was dancing, and Oumid had drawn himself in the background playing his flute. Could it be that the keegrah spoke the truth – that Oumid could speak to the demons and they would listen? This demon clearly was listening to the flute.

If this was an accurate picture – everything he'd heard from every source suggested that the keegrah didn't lie, perhaps even did not know how to lie. This was subversive; it turned a major part of grehti dogma

on its head. If it was an accurate picture, then the demon
– the girl in the picture – could communicate, at least by
reacting to the music, by dancing. It was communicating
with Oumid. If they could prove it, then there could be
weapons created – no. Not weapons. The demons could
be soothed, perhaps even repelled. The shashigai stroked
his beard, deep in thought. The demons did nothing but
kill. It would be a weapon, then. And no one in their
right mind would leave a demon alive. It was no wonder
that Oumid wanted his privacy. He was in love with this
demon – to him, she was the sky. If the grehti found out
– well, they wouldn't. Nishom should know; the
shashigai would tell the nethik since he was likely to have
the most contact with Oumid in the future. His sources
had told him that Nishom could be trusted with such
information, though it was likely that the nethik already
knew. The nethik probably knew more about the
demons than anyone else, since they lived in the forests
where the most demons lurked.

The shashigai continued to study the picture. It
would need to be kept hidden or destroyed, and the
keegrah would need to be told that he should not draw
such things.

The picture called into question the things they
called demon, and also the judgment of the grehti, who
condemned to death anyone at risk of becoming a
demon. If a demon could speak, then they could learn its
nature. For some reason this one had not harmed
Oumid. Zev smiled. Actually, the reason was clear. The

nethik had taught Oumid to paint and he had learned the craft well. The painting was far from crude. There was an expression of joy, of love, on the face of the sperith. She was in love, with Oumid, or his music, or both.

There was also the question of why the other speritu did not attack Oumid, but this mystery could be solved too. The demons fed on people with strong emotion, and Oumid was the opposite of that. What strong emotions he had were probably pleasure and not much more. Not only that, but because Oumid saw the demons as people, he wasn't afraid of them.

He sighed. He had promised to let Oumid go after he'd told his story. But there was so much more to be learned. If the sperith could speak to Oumid, perhaps it could speak to Zev. He pulled thoughtfully on his beard, and decided to eavesdrop on the events going on in the tent where he'd sent Oumid. After that, he might be able to convince Oumid to stay and elaborate on some of the things in his story.

It was too late for spying. The meeting in the tent was done. Oumid emerged from the tent smiling (for the first time since he had left his mountain), and behind him came a man with long braided hair, but clean shaven like a nethik, laughing. The man clapped Oumid's shoulder, then turned grinning and said to Zev, "Well? Is he not what I told you? I said you would have to show me to him to convince him to stay. He did not believe it was me, until I showed him my shield and greeted him in the manner of Akhad Rai."

"Then he will stay and talk to us?" asked Zev.

"So long as you let him have his sky," laughed Al-Medi. "Every day he will want to go to the highest place and play his flute for the sky."

"That is a good arrangement," said Zev. "I am eager to meet his sky."

That caused Al-Medi to look confused.

"In time," smiled Zev. "First we need to make sure that this keegrah cannot tell anyone that you are here. Even with your disguise, there would be danger. We should touch him to close his mind to any probing."

Al-Medi smiled. "You don't need to touch his mind. I have told him that he cannot tell anyone where Al-Medi is, and he can do that." Al-Medi rolled his eyes. "I know from experience."

He turned to Oumid and said, "Where is Al-Medi?"

Oumid looked at Al-Medi, then looked confused for a moment and finally said, "I cannot say."

"You ask him," said Al-Medi to the shashigai.

"Where is Al-Medi?" asked Zev.

"I cannot say."

"Do you mean that you know where he is, and cannot tell me?"

Oumid looked thoughtful for a moment, then replied, "No, I mean that I cannot say."

Zev scratched his head.

"Al-Medi is standing next to you. Can you see him?"

"I cannot say."

"Are you blind?"

"No, I am not."

"All right," said the shashigai, "That's enough. You don't have to pretend you don't know. In this camp you can say that you saw Al-Medi."

"No," said Oumid, "I cannot."

Zev closed his eyes and concentrated. In addition to being a shashigai he was indeed a grehti, and with telepathy he could look into Oumid's mind and see if Oumid could hide the truth that Al-Medi was alive and hiding in the caravan of the shashigai.

It was like trying to move a hauling taralk. He probed this way and that, and Oumid's mind yielded nothing. The keegrah's thoughts were both scattered and clouded. Time passed, and finally Zev opened his eyes. He had a pounding headache, and Oumid was looking at him curiously.

"Are you hurt?" asked the keegrah. Al-Medi was roaring with laughter in the background.

"Well," said Zev, "I guess he really can't tell."

Al-Medi shrugged. "It is the way his mind works. He needs no wards. Anyone who tries to touch his mind will have a headache."

"From experience?"

Al-Medi grinned. "He was my student."

Later, while most of the caravan slept, there was another meeting.

Two men sat at one of the night fires, drinking ruka and talking. The fire guard had left them to tend the fire, so they were alone.

Zev stroked his beard.

"It may be that they will come after him anyway."

Al-Medi nodded.

"What can be done? Even Akhad Rai can buy only so many reckoners."

"I'll send word to the other shashigai. My brothers and I will think of something."

Al-Medi grinned.

"You are the shashigai – I expect you will."

CHAPTER 25
Oumid Is Not Here

The rsakk Cailtoh was important. He was head of research at Eileah. He was affiliated with the house of the Tapestry Master at Tuklos, and he was rich. He had brought with him bribes, and if those failed to influence the nethik elder of the forest below Cnieren, then the rsakk and keegrah warriors surely would make the nethik Nishom talk.

Nishom, the elder of the village, had the distinction of being grehti as well as shashigai. The shashigai primarily were storytellers, but so good at their craft that many villages used them as historians. This made them valuable to the grehti, who made them allies but did not train them in the ways of the grehti. They did not, after all, have the requisite mind powers.

However, some, like Nishom, initially had been trained grehti and later had been recruited into the patchwork tribe of the shashigai, whose only membership criteria were a good memory and a talent for embellishment of historical details. Children of the shashigai tribes were trained in memory and storytelling techniques, and the ones who displayed mind powers were taken to Eileah and trained there. Like the rsakk, the shashigai's allegiance was primarily to their tribe, so trust was an issue.

The issue of trust was what had prompted High Grehti Cailtoh to bring military force with him to the nethik village. His soldiers had searched the village, but there was no sign of the keegrah rumored to be able to talk to the demons. High Grehti Cailtoh needed that keegrah. Having Marai at Eileah had been useless – the demon she called only attacked her and never stayed long enough to be trapped. High Grehti Cailtoh did not believe the second rumor that had reached him while he was searching for the fellow – that during an attempt to communicate with the speritu, one of the demons had touched him and he had fallen from the sky.

The event had been witnessed by residents of the keegrah village at Cnieren, including its elder, and by some of the residents of the nethik village.

The event had been staged.

It was too convenient. High Grehti Cailtoh was being hindered at every step of his path to harnessing the power of the demons. First the woman who'd held the gem he'd needed had died before she could bring it to him, and then the gem had been returned to the cowardly elders of Tuklos, who had thrown it into the pit fire at Ak-Shamalim, or lost it in the desert. He'd heard both things from Ak-Shamalim. And then by order of the elders of Eileah, he'd had to personally escort Marai back to the portal that took her away from Karn forever.

High Grehti Cailtoh had seen Marai back to her world, where she was safely hidden away from Karnese demons. He had been unable to sway the council at Eileah in their decision to send her back to the polluted place she'd come from. She had left before he could employ more persuasive means to get through her wards. His next plan had been to gather information from those who had been near her at Ak-Shamalim.

But Al-Medi, the former head of Ak-Shamalim, had vanished into the badlands, aided either by the rogue Akhad Rai, or the shashigai, or both. No matter, he'd thought. There was still Oumid, the simple-minded keegrah who'd been Al-Medi's student and Marai's friend. It was rumored that he could not only call the demons, but that he could communicate with them. Even Marai had not been able to do that.

High Grehti Cailtoh had been on his way to question the fellow when some keegrah had come from the mountains – they were supposed to report on the location of Oumid, who favored the high mountains above Cnieren. The shashigai had made an agreement with Oumid that the grehti would not call on him to perform services again, and the keegrah had retired to the almost inaccessible parts of those mountains.

High Grehti Cailtoh of Eileah was not bound by shashigai promises. He didn't need the keegrah to work – he wanted the fellow's mind.

Nishom offered him a cup of ruka – High Grehti Cailtoh brushed it away, knocking the cup to the ground.

"I do not have time for formalities. I want to see the place where the keegrah fell. I want to see the body."

Nishom picked up the cup. There was a muddy spot where the ruka had sunk into the ground, and he regarded it thoughtfully.

"I could send you with some guides –"

"Just tell me the location – I have my own soldiers, keegrah warriors and trackers. They will find it."

"There may not be much left – keegrah meat is highly prized by some."

"Then we will find the trail of those who took him. Show me the location."

Nishom sighed.

"I will describe it to your men. Your keegrah will be able to find his camp. It has not been disturbed because the speritu were involved. He fell close to there."

High Grehti Cailtoh stalked out of the tent. He was sure that the nethik was lying to him.

Nonetheless, they set out for the mountain. When they reached Cnieren, High Grehti Cailtoh called for the captain of his squad of assassins. He gave the captain instructions to burn the nethik village from which they had come.

"Master," said the captain, "The grehti will not like that. The elder Nishom is full grehti."

"Fool!" said High Grehti Cailtoh, "I didn't say kill *him*! Kill anyone who tries to stop you, but leave the grehti alone. He knows better than to stand in my way. Let him watch and suffer as his village is destroyed. The nethik are our slaves. The grehti cannot object to the natural order of things. These slaves have defied me. Burn their homes – kill anyone who tries to stop you. Do what you want with the women. Then kill everyone except the grehti. This is their punishment."

The captain gave acknowledgement. High Grehti Cailtoh and his men had been traveling in nok toward the place where Oumid had fallen. The captain and his squad took their shapes and went back along the trail to the nethik village. It would be easy enough. The homes in the village were constructed of skins and sticks – not baked clay as in Tuklos, or cut stone as in places like Cnieren and Eileah. The village would burn easily.

High Grehti Cailtoh went to question the elder of Cnieren.

Cnieren was a remote place – so remote that they had trouble finding grehti to stay there. The village had nothing but stone and metal ore to offer. Some went there to trade, but most waited at the nethik village for the keegrah to haul their wagons of ore down the mountain path. The elder had been in the village for many years – he was old and his health was failing. He'd pose no obstacle to High Grehti Cailtoh's probing. He was one of the keegrah who'd seen Oumid fall.

The interview left High Grehti Cailtoh in a foul mood. Apparently the Cnieren keegrah had flown out to investigate what the elder had seen. They reported a body down in the trees below Oumid's camp. The facts were clear. High Grehti Cailtoh wondered if the shashigai had arranged to kill the keegrah so that his secrets would not be exposed. It was possible.

No. Not unless the keegrah had given away his secrets, and from what he'd heard, the fellow was well warded. No. They were hiding him. He'd find out. He smiled to himself. Perhaps Nishom would talk – when he saw his village burning and his people sacrificed, he'd talk.

He ordered his men to march – they would have to go along the next part in nok – the forest was becoming less and less friendly to rsakk-shape. They had enough weapons and skill. No one would challenge them. He would find the keegrah, look into his mind, and then bring him back to Eileah for the grehti to study.

As High Grehti Cailtoh had instructed, the captain and his squad of assassins waited until night, and then rushed into the nethik village with torches and war cries.

They stopped in amazement.

The village was gone.

They had scouted it before sunset – the people had been moving about in innocence, not knowing their fate. There had been smoke from fires and the smells of cooking. Children had been running about.

Now there was no sign, save the beaten ground, that there had been any humans living there at all.

The captain sighed.

High Grehti Cailtoh was going to be unhappy.

High Grehti Cailtoh was very unhappy. The trackers had found the corpse – what was left of it. The meat was gone and the bones were scattered – and there weren't many. The trackers confirmed that it was a keegrah. There were still some feathers about. It would be hard to tell if it was the right keegrah, but the trackers told him that the signs indicated someone had fallen about the same time as it had been reported that the Ak-Shamalim keegrah had fallen. They packed up what was left of the keegrah and prepared to go back to Cnieren. Even with rsakkfire to protect them, the night forest would be dark and dangerous, and there had been demon sightings.

The shashigai had been telling the truth. The keegrah had fallen to his death here.

High Grehti Cailtoh's mood was helped a little by the thought of the nethik village burning and the elder Nishom watching his women raped and killed. He looked forward to meeting the captain of his assassin squad on their way out of the forest.

CHAPTER 26
Healing

Nethik carriers arrived in a part of the forest that was inaccessible unless one knew both the marks that indicated the narrow trail and how to negotiate the ankle-wrenching rocks there that slid over each other and made it almost impossible to travel without surefooted hooves.

They set up a new village within hours.

The clearing where they set up the village was already occupied – high in the trees there was a platform, and on the platform, a grumbling tirothi elder had been sewing.

Her name was T'noui, and she was not a seamstress, but rather, a surgeon.

Her patient was a keegrah who had fallen through some trees after tumbling down the side of a mountain.

She'd sewn him back together, and in a few moons he would be flying through the sky, good as young.

Nishom climbed up to see the patient.

"He hasn't said a word," T'noui grumbled.

"You were warned about that," said Nishom, and to Oumid, he said, "How are you?"

The keegrah didn't answer.

Nishom smiled. "I have something for you – I had my scouts get it when you fell."

"Idiots!" grumbled T'noui, as Nishom handed Oumid his flute.

Oumid's face lit up. He put the flute to his lips, and T'noui snatched it away.

"You can't have that - you're going to bust my stitches! And you're not bringing any demons here! Understand?"

Oumid looked penitent.

Nishom laughed.

"There's your talk," he said.

"Hmph! All this just to make one grehti go away! What if this one had got killed? Or worse, what if he really got touched by a demon?"

"But," said Nishom, "he's not, and he didn't, and you've made him good as new."

T'noui continued to grumble, but she stroked Oumid's head. She had been told what he and Marai had done for Chaipa, her daughter.

Nishom took the flute out of T'noui's hands.

"May I?"

The question was directed at Oumid, who nodded, and whose eyes closed as Nishom began to play the melody Oumid/Kgh'jsh loved, the one that had bound Oumid to the sky, the demon sister of Marai - the rich, measured notes of the fire dance.

GLOSSARY

A

Abadran-rsakk – One of the first four shapefinders.
Ak-Shamalim – A shapehouse mainly for rsakk and keegrah. A training school for grehti is also located there.
Akhad Rai – A bandit turned merchant. He commands a sizable military force which grew as a result of raids on bandit camps. He is related to Marai, but distantly.
Al-Medi – The head of Ak-Shamalim, a grehti.

B

Bonnus – Marai's love interest in Dekan.

C

Cailtoh – Elder of Eileah; head of research.

Chaipa – A princess raised in the tirothi race but of the rsakk after her shapefinding.

Cnieren – A mining town in the k'g'hrah mountains. They mine iron there, though there have been rumors of jewels found in the mountains.

Common - The language used for communication between shapes. A variant of nethik tongue.

D

Dekan – Marai's home town, located on another world called Beren Gan, accessible via a portal in the desert west and south of Ak-Shamalim. Specific and powerful magic is needed to use the portal.

Dekani – Lowest caste of the three tribes of Tuklos. The Dekani provide services to the rest of the rsakk, including what amount to bounty hunters, who will track prey until they find it, or until they, the hunters, are killed (see reckoners).

E

Eileah – The elite school of the grehti, and the location of the standing stones, a sacred relic of the grehti.

Elder - One of the wise and experienced leaders of a tribe.

Esgeni – A tribe of Tuklos. They are traders and merchants; they trade mostly in jewels and tools.

Esh – A mixed shapehouse near Eileah. K'g'hrah and nethik train there.

Ethkell – Major trade city in Karn. It is centrally located between the keegrah mountains in the north and the tirothi jungles in the west. There is a river alongside the city, and on the other side of the river, a keegrah military camp is under construction.

G

Garad – Leader of the k'g'hrah military at Ak-Shamalim.
Grehti – The priests of the Shapefinding and stewards of the Change, chosen by the Mother to protect the knowledge of the four sacred shapes.

H

Hsora-rsakk the Strong - One of the first grehti.

K

Karn – The world in which Oumid lives.
Keegrah (common for K'g'hrah) – Second of the four sacred shapes. A winged and furred bird creature with a beak not unlike an eagle's.
Kilani of the nethik – One of the first four shapefinders.

M

Marai – Fourteen-year-old newfound from Dekan.
Merinell – A nethik farming village destroyed by demons.

Mother – A woman who cares for children or who has a leadership role among women. The wife of an elder. A female grehti.

Mother, the – The grehti teach that all created things emerge from the Mother. Basis of the tirothi religion.

Mother Shiri – Al-Medi's first wife; in charge of training the women at Ak-Shamalim.

N

Nethik – Fourth of the four sacred shapes. Fey, horned herd beasts who live on the plains and in the light woods. Often enslaved by the rsakk.

Nishom – A nethik storyteller of the tribe of the shashigai. His village (named for him) is close to Cnieren.

Nok – The human form of a Karnese shapeshifter.

R

Reckoners – Fierce rsakk bounty hunters known for the speed of their pursuit. They are known to resort to extreme measures to capture the hunted. Their tracking skill is as legendary as their creative use of violence.

Rsakk – First of the four shapes. Flightless lizards with fire breath who mostly live in the southern badlands.

S

Sarkoth – A feline predator that hunts both other animals and humans.

Sean-grah – One of the first four shapefinders.

Sh'tai of the tirothi – One of the first four shapefinders.

Shape – The grehti teach that there are four shapes sacred to the Mother: the rsakk who are like lizards and breathe fire, the k'g'hrah who are like birds, the tirothi who are covered with fur and swing in trees, and the nethik who are like taralk.

Shapefinder – A grehti priest who facilitates the shapefinding of boys and girls who have counted fourteen summers.

Shapebound – One who by magic is rendered unable to shift from nok to one's shape, or conversely, unable to shift back to nok.

Shapehouse – A place where experienced teachers train newly shapefound (newfound) men and women to use their shapes. Since the process is often traumatic, the shapehouses are removed from the villages. Trades are also taught at shapehouse.

Shapesick – Unable to change shape or stuck between nok and one's sacred shape.

Shashigai – A tribe of storytellers made up of people from all shapes. They go to the various towns and tribes and gather stories both to entertain and to teach. The stories are brought back to one of many locations where they are woven into tapestries (rsakk and nethik) or painted on cave walls (rsakk and keegrah).

Shavadi – A grehti and an opportunist, which he thinks makes him a good businessman. He did most of his "business" with the new girls that came to Ak-Shamalim.

Stripefur – A rabbit-like creature with a dark stripe running the length of its body and tail.

T

T'noui – Grehti, elder tirothi (wife of a Sender) and mother of Chaipa.

Tapestry Master – Historian and leader of the rsakk at Tuklos, who are an alliance of three tribes – the Vahtani, who consider themselves the rightful rulers of all of Karn, the Esgeni, who are traders in jewels, findings and weapons, and the Dekani, who are outcasts but who do the dirty work of the other tribes. They are allowed to live within the city walls, but in a separate section.

Taralk – Any number of four-footed, hoofed animals including things that look like cows, things that look like deer, and all sizes of things in between. There are milk taralk and grass-eating taralk. At one point the nethik were included in the classification "taralk" but one of their tribes objected since they had been identified by the grehti as one of the sacred shapes. Nethik was the name of the tribe of record, therefore all taralk which could shift to nok became known as nethik.

Tiroth – Third of the four shapes. Playful, dexterous monkeylike beings with poison fangs and a penchant for sweet fruits.

The Tizzy – An inn in the city of Dekan, Marai's home town.

Tollach – The k'g'hrah shapehouse where Oumid went when he left Ak-Shamalim.

Tuklos – Major trade city in the south region of Karn. Dominated by rsakk.

Y

Yaida – Al-Medi's third (promoted to second) wife; actually a wife in training.

Wolf Tinker

In another place and time, he might be called autistic. After years as a counselor, navigating social interaction and political intrigue, he's retreated to a place he will not reveal, where he hopes to mend instead of melt down. Wolf Tinker is a storyteller who, when he is not surfing his beloved internet, takes human form to tell his tales. For years after writing his first tale at the age of ten, he wandered in search of a world in which to find his stories. That place is Karn, a world of demons, shapeshifters and magic-wielding priests. He hopes you will enjoy your adventures there as much as he has.

Joanna Erbach

Joanna is an artist, firebug, and lizardwoman who lives with one foot in the Dreaming. She has been illustrating for fantasy and science fiction projects since 2000, and has worked with authors such as Edward Bryant, Connie Willis, Brian Herbert and Kevin J. Anderson. When not working on art, she divides her time between rock climbing, gaming, and studying the strange and complex phenomenon that is the human race.

www.ingramcontent.com/pod-product-compliance
Lightning Source LLC
Chambersburg PA
CBHW071149170626
46809CB00002B/836